DEATH IN A HURRY

Death in a Hurry

A Patrick Dawlish Mystery

John Creasey *writing as* Gordon Ashe

OPEN ROAD
INTEGRATED MEDIA
NEW YORK

Copyright © 1952 by Gordon Ashe

ISBN: 978-1-5040-9809-0

This edition published in 2024 by Open Road Integrated Media, Inc.
180 Maiden Lane
New York, NY 10038
www.openroadmedia.com

DEATH IN A HURRY

ONE

DISMAY FOR DAWLISH

"Darling!" called Felicity Dawlish.

There was no answer.

"*Dar*ling!" repeated Felicity, and could not keep the excitement out of her voice.

She stood by the open front door of the Dawlish's house near Haslemere, in Surrey, with the lovely green of the English countryside stretched out in front of her. She gazed over the lawn to the meadows and trees beyond. A soft breeze blew in from the south-west, rustling the letter in her hand, her light-brown hair and the linen flowered house-coat she was wearing.

She continued to read the letter, and cried again:

"*Darrr-ling!*"

There was still no answer.

She finished reading and folded the letter; the gay red-and-blue markings on the edges showed that it was an air-letter from a country with brighter postal ideas than England.

She turned to the stairs.

"Pat, where are you?"

Her husband did not answer, yet she knew he was upstairs.

She had seen him go ten minutes before the postman had cycled up the steep drive to the timbered, pseudo-Elizabethan house. Its name, Four Ways, came from the narrow roads which intersected a few hundred yards from the gates.

Felicity hurried up the stairs.

"Pat," she cried, "where are you?"

There was still no answer.

She frowned, looked into the spacious modern bathroom, hurried into the bedroom, and went across to the window, which overlooked Four Ways' thirty acres, mostly planted with apple- and plum-trees; for Patrick Dawlish was by way of being an amateur fruit farmer. Just in sight was that patch of the grounds set aside for the pigs; fine fat English bacon pigs. Three were in sight, snouts lowered to the ground.

Felicity didn't see her husband.

"Where on earth—" she began.

"Beware of a woman with excitement in her voice, for you may be sure that she desires more than you are prepared to give," boomed a deep voice, startling her so that she swung round. "Doubly beware of the woman who runs upstairs fluttering a letter of ill-omen. Were you calling?"

"Fool," said Felicity roundly.

Dawlish stood behind the door, his big face almost handsome but spoiled by a broken nose, and looking sombre now with a mock scowl. He had corn-coloured hair, short, crisp, and wavy, a massive chin with a cleft, eyes as blue as the sky on a summer morning. He was huge, six feet three in his stockinged feet, with massive shoulders. Fourteen hours a day spent in the open air had tanned his cheeks and arms. He wore a pale-blue, short-sleeved shirt and a pair of well-pressed flannel trousers on this warm morning in September.

"No," said Dawlish.

4

"No, what?"

"That's the answer to whatever you were going to ask. It's impossible."

"Idiot," said Felicity, and went across, still holding the letter. The gaiety was back in her eyes, and she looked fresh and lovely. "Pat, do you remember—"

"Your uncle in America," said Dawlish.

Felicity started, and frowned.

"How did you know it was about him?" she asked, in a tone which suggested that she really didn't believe that he had mentioned an uncle or America. "You can't have. You—"

"The next stage will be trying to convince me that pigs don't make bacon." Dawlish stepped forward, moved suddenly, pinioned her arms and lifted her effortlessly until her nose was on a level with his; he had to raise her five inches off the ground. Gravely he rubbed noses, and put her down. "They do, and that's from your legendary Uncle Sam."

"His name isn't Sam, it's Zeb, but—" She broke off, looking at him thoughtfully. "I wish you weren't so bright," she said half-seriously.

"Bright? I'm not bright. I'm a country bumpkin, remember? When you wanted to go to Paris and I wanted to stay at home, I was a rural dullard without imagination. All I was fit for was picking up the windfalls and feeding the pigs with them."

"*That's* true, too, but I'm glad we didn't go, because—"

"Uncle Zeb's on his way," groaned Dawlish.

Felicity went across to the large double bed and sat down, looking at him with thoughtful eyes. He had a mind that could be as quick as light, she knew only too well. He loved the simple ease of the country, but it wasn't really his life. Occasionally he would break out in some fierce, furious spell of action. This was the man who might wake one sunny morning to a day which promised no excitements, and by nightfall be in the headlines of every newspaper, setting police, Press, and public by the ears.

"Tell me," ordered Felicity.

"Yes, ma'am. I looked out of the window and saw Bill Morgan strolling up, having left his bike at the gates. He had one letter in his hand. It was all colours of the rainbow round the edges, and that meant South Africa or the United States, and—shall I go on?"

"Yes."

"Yes, *ma'am*. We seldom get letters from either place, and only last week you were being sad because you hadn't heard from Uncle Sam—"

"Zeb."

"Yes, dear. For over six months. You met Bill Morgan at the door, and instead of indulging in idle village gossip, took one glance at the letter, gave him an apple and sent him packing. Then you really became excited. Now why should you get really excited because of a letter from Uncle Zed?"

"Zeb. I see how your mind worked. Pat, they *are* coming."

Dawlish looked as if iced water had been poured over him.

"*They?*"

"Uncle Zeb, Elvira, and Homer."

"Oh," said Dawlish faintly. "Quite a family party. We'll send them a letter and tell them how nice it would have been to see them, and what a pity it is we're in Paris!"

"Brute." Felicity stood up, and looked a little anxious. "Darling, you won't really be difficult, will you?"

Dawlish chuckled.

"No, my sweet." He squeezed Felicity's waist, and she gasped. "I'm just a little nervous of Uncle Zeb and his two offspring, because—"

"Just because he's made money!"

"Oh, no. That's still legal in America."

"Because he made a *lot* of money."

"Wrong. Because he will be high-pressured, judging from his letters. I feel in a lethargic mood. And there's just one disturbing thing about Uncle Zeb."

"What?"

"Why christen a girl Elvira and a boy Homer?"

"That was probably his wife. I never liked Aunt Kate. Any how—"

"How old are they?"

"About twenty, I think, perhaps a little more."

"And Zeb?"

"I'm not sure. About fifty, I suppose." Felicity went to the dressing-table, sat down, and began to make-up. "It doesn't matter how old he is, and I think you'll like him. The youngsters will probably want to be off on their own most of the time, so you needn't worry about them. Going to read the letter?"

"Need I?"

"Not if you don't want to," said Felicity. "Darling, be a pet and get my green suit out of the spare-room wardrobe, will you?"

"Which green suit?"

"The light-green one. I've only two, and you know the other one's almost worn out."

"It's good for a long time yet!" Dawlish went out, and Felicity's eyes laughed at herself in the mirror, but she was looking demure again when Dawlish came back with the suit on a padded hanger. He took it off and put it on the bed, while Felicity stood up, slipped out of the house-coat, and reminded him that she had a lovely figure, and a nice taste in lingerie.

"Not bad," said Dawlish. "Why are you dressing yourself up?"

"I want to be at my best," said Felicity.

The dawning of a frown wrinkled Dawlish's forehead. He put

his head on one side, then went across to the dressing-table and picked up the letter. It was actually from Elvira Deverall. Dawlish scanned it until he reached the last paragraph, when Felicity interrupted.

"Isn't Elvira sweet? She's so anxious to see us that she won't let the others spend any time in London first. Uncle Zeb's got a Daimler hire, meeting them at the airport, and will come straight down here. The plane is due at London Airport at ten o'clock on Thursday, September the seventeenth. Say half an hour for Customs and an hour and a half at most for the journey, and they'll be here by twelve. It *is* Thursday the seventeenth, isn't it?"

Dawlish breathed heavily.

"It is. And it is twenty-two minutes to twelve."

"So I had to dress quickly, didn't I?" asked Felicity. "I—Pat, listen!" She ran across to the window and leaned out—and pointed. "Pat, there's a big car coming this way, they're here!"

She ran back to the bed.

"Do me up at the back, quickly!"

Dawlish applied himself to yellow buttons. Felicity swung round, as soon as he had finished, and hurried out of the room. The large car, a black Daimler, was already turning into the drive. Dawlish watched it, but from this height could not see the driver or the passengers clearly.

He did see a small open two-seater, also black, which passed the end of the drive, went up the gentle hill for a hundred yards, then disappeared behind some trees. He waited at the window as the big car stopped. Felicity cried a welcome, and American voices answered.

The little black two-seater stayed hidden by the trees; which meant that it had stopped. Absently he wondered why; then he turned to the door.

TWO

WELCOME

"Hallo, hallo, hallo," boomed Dawlish, and ran down the stairs towards the group of four. Felicity was just inside the hall, a tall, well-built man wearing a wide-brimmed hat was holding her hand, a bare-headed youth with startlingly black hair stood by a girl whose hair was as startling, but red. Dawlish did not give himself time to do more than notice that the red-headed Elvira would create a sensation in most male circles before he went forward and gripped the older man's hands.

"Well, well, Uncle Sam! This is delightful. Wonderful to see you! Come in, come in! And—*Homer!*" He gripped Homer's hand; his was double the other's size, for Homer was much smaller than his father. "Welcome to the English countryside." He turned. "*Elvira!*" he breathed, took both her hands, pulled her to him, and kissed her warmly on each cheek. "Now! What about a little drink, honey? I think I put the champagne in the ice-box, but if I didn't it's still in the pantry. Come on, now."

He put his arm round Elvira's waist, slid his other arm through Felicity's uncle's, and led the way into the big drawing-room.

Uncle Zeb said slowly, "You're very kind, Mr. Dawlish."

9

"Oh, shucks. Shush, I mean. No formality, please. Pat, or if you really prefer it, Patrick. Felicity only calls me Patrick when she's cross. Eh Fel?"

"Yes, *Patrick*," said Felicity tartly.

"She doesn't mean it this time, it's only a joke," explained Dawlish.

"I've heard a lot about the English sense of humour," said Uncle Zeb, still slowly. He had a low-pitched, rather husky voice, which marked him as from the South. He also had a pair of fine grey eyes, and they were twinkling. His face was lean and clean cut, and he gave an impression of strength and confidence. "I guess I'll learn more about it in the next few weeks. Don't you, Homer?"

Homer, who was looking at Dawlish with his head on one side and his eyes narrowed, had a voice which to English ears was only slightly American.

"It wouldn't surprise me, Dad. I think I'm going to enjoy my researches into the English sense of humour. That's if Cousin Pat will be my tutor."

"But he can't be that," cried Elvira. "He's mine. I just don't care what Felicity says, he's going to show me around, I just *have* to have a chaperone."

Dawlish chuckled.

"I think we're going to get along nicely."

"I certainly hope so," said Uncle Zeb. "We've heard so much about you from Felicity, in her letters, and we've also read about you in the newspapers. You can thank Homer for that, he's a newspaperman, and he reads the English newspapers regularly."

"Oh," said Dawlish. "That's hard."

"We know plenty about you," said Homer, grinning. "The good and the bad."

"If you ask Felicity at the moment, it will be nearly all bad," said Dawlish.

"You needn't think anything you say is going to stop you from taking me around." Elvira's eyes were dancing. "Felicity will just have to lend you to me for a while. Do you mind, Felicity?"

She looked at the door as Felicity came in, carrying two bottles of champagne on a silver tray.

"I'll give him to you gladly," said Felicity. She glanced round quickly, saw the ease of their expressions and laughed. "Pat's a hopeless fool, and doesn't realize that sometimes he might be taken seriously."

"We won't take him seriously," promised Homer.

"Let me open those bottles and get to business," said Dawlish.

While Felicity set out the glasses, he released the corks expertly. They popped loudly, and he poured out. Felicity carried the glasses round.

The visitors still wore their coats, and the car in which they had arrived was outside—Felicity had doubtless sent the chauffeur round to the back for refreshments.

Dawlish moved towards the window and glanced out now and again. He could see the trees where the small car had disappeared, but could not see the car. Once he frowned, but that quickly disappeared and he went on talking lightly. The inimitable gift, given to many Americans but to few English, of becoming immediately at home, made this a friendly party; it could be fun for the next week or two.

Dawlish glanced out of the window again.

A man moved from behind a bush, swiftly, furtively. He was about fifty yards from the house, and on the side of the drive nearer the clump of trees. He was dressed in a brown suit, and wore a hat pulled low over his eyes. When Dawlish looked again there was no sign of him.

Elvira was saying, "Is it really true that Scotland Yard consults you, Pat? You're a private detective, who—"

"No!" Dawlish looked pained. "An amateur with a long nose and a habit of getting mixed up in troubles. I've a good friend at the Yard, you'll have to meet him—care to go over the place with me?"

"Can you fix *that*?"

"I think so."

"In New York they think you're the best private eye in England," said Homer handsomely.

"That's true," Uncle Zeb confirmed, and seemed amused.

"Just a build-up. Forget it."

Elvira clapped her hands together and laughed.

"He *is* English, after all. It doesn't matter how he tries to fool us, he's as English as they come. See how modest he is? Felicity, why do you let him hide his light under a bushel?"

"Hide it? He'd set any bushel alight!"

"Happily married, too," jeered Homer.

"I suggest we get to know each other a little more before we start treading on corns we don't know the others have got," drawled Uncle Zeb.

"Now that's a good idea." Felicity drained her glass, and turned to Elvira. "Let's get upstairs, I'll show you to your room and you can start unpacking. Uncle Zeb, will you and Homer mind sharing—"

"We can't all stay with you in that way, Felicity. It's very good of you, but we just wanted to come and say hallo before finding a hotel. We can get to London in an hour and—"

"You will stay here," said Dawlish firmly.

The man outside had appeared twice again, and was now only thirty yards from the house. Dawlish turned and stood with his back to the window looking on to the drive.

"Yes, of course," said Felicity. "Come along, Elvira."

"Well, if you're sure."

"I'm positive. I'll get our handyman to take the cases upstairs."

"You're so very kind."

Elvira followed Felicity out, and Dawlish, still with his back to the window, moved backward a foot, glanced at the door, and spoke very quietly:

"Shut the door, Homer, will you?"

Homer said, "Surely." He moved across, closed the door and stared at Dawlish with puzzled eyes. His father looked puzzled, too. They had reason, for Dawlish's expression had changed. The smile had gone, and there was a wooden look about him that was almost inane. He didn't move from the window, but said softly:

"I don't want to alarm the girls yet."

"Alarm—" began Homer, and broke off.

"Yes. Listen. I don't yet know why you've come, and I'm glad you're here, but I don't like your friends. There's at least one man in the garden, not thirty yards away. He's wearing an American-cut suit, and he doesn't want to be seen. There may be another. Anyone gunning for you?"

The last words came out abruptly.

Uncle Zeb said hoarsely, "*No!*"

He didn't mean that no one was gunning for them.

"You mean this?" Homer's voice was sharp.

"Yes. You were followed in a smaller car. Did you notice it?"

"I can't say I did."

Homer moved towards the window, but before he reached it his father said in a tense voice:

"Be careful, Homer."

Homer stopped.

"So it's like that," said Dawlish.

It was so improbable that it was almost fantastic; but these men were alarmed. The presence of the man outside did not surprise them. They were shocked, especially Uncle Zeb, by the confirmation of danger, and not surprised that there was any. A dozen questions boiled in Dawlish's mind, but this wasn't the time to voice them. He waited, long enough for either of the others to protest, to say that it was absurd to suggest they had been followed; and when neither did, he knew beyond all doubt that it was true.

He said, "You two aren't carrying guns, are you?"

"I am," said Homer briefly. "I smuggled it through."

"Well, don't try to smuggle it out again. If it's necessary, I'll get you a licence. It'll have to be proved necessary. If you should have to use it, say you borrowed it from me."

Dawlish's voice was quiet but firm. He assumed command quite naturally, and in this mood would take it for granted that the others would accept all he said.

"You, Uncle Zeb?"

"I don't carry one."

"Then you'd better come with me. Homer, stay in this room, keep close to the wall by this window, and watch. Don't start any fireworks, this might only be an errand of inquiry. Uncle Zeb, will you follow me? There's an attic room with dormer windows, and we can look down and see how many visitors we have in the garden. We'll have to pass the girls, but they'll probably be so busy with clothes they won't notice."

The two older men went out, and Dawlish nodded to Riddle, their handyman, who was coming down the stairs; all the cases had disappeared from the hall.

"See you later," Dawlish said.

"Yes, sir."

Felicity and Elvira were talking nineteen to the dozen. In

a mirror Dawlish caught sight of Felicity holding a dress up in front of her. He grinned again as he led the way across the landing to the second staircase, a narrow one which led up to the attic rooms. A small landing had been built up there, and there were two bedrooms, one used by the maid.

They reached a doorway.

"Want the police to know about this yet?" asked Dawlish lightly.

"No, Pat." Zebadiah looked most uneasy.

"It may have to happen." Dawlish led the way to a dormer window, which overlooked the garden, the drive, and the rolling countryside. He could see the trees but not the car. By leaning close to the window, he could also see the back of the bushes which lined the drive—and the top of a hat. The man he had seen was still about twenty yards from the house, and in line with the window which Homer was guarding. No one else appeared to be in sight.

Uncle Zeb came forward, and peered out.

He didn't speak.

"This way," said Dawlish.

He led the way out of this room to the next. Here the window overlooked the back garden; there was a better view of the piggery and the orchard. They could also see the vegetable-garden and more bush fruit-trees and huge soft-fruit bushes, in wire cages. No one was in sight.

"Would you expect one man by himself?" asked Dawlish.

"No."

"Then we ought to find out where his companion's gone," said Dawlish. He turned to the doorway, and shot Uncle Zeb a quick grin. "Felicity loves you at the moment, but when she knows you've started me on a mystery march, she'll lose a lot of her enthusiasm—at first. She'll soon come round."

Uncle Zeb said, "You're certainly cool, Pat."

"Why get excited?" asked Dawlish, at the head of the stairs. "I should think—"

He didn't say what he would think, for a scream broke the quiet of the house, sounding high above the voices of Felicity and Elvira. It came again, as Dawlish raced down the stairs, past a startled Felicity, who stood in the doorway of the spare room.

A third scream came from the kitchen as he reached the hall, and Homer appeared, gun in hand.

THREE

CHASE

Dawlish reached the kitchen, with Homer close behind him. A pair of bare legs with pale, massive calves were waving wildly in the air. One foot was bare; a black shoe hung on the other. Two hands, belonging to Ethel the cook-general, were clutching at a chair. Ethel's head and shoulders touched the floor, and she was struggling to get up. As Dawlish glanced at her she gave another piercing scream.

Footsteps thudded in the garden.

"A man!" screamed Ethel. "A man! Gun!"

Dawlish reached the back door in time to see a man clearing the wire fence round the piggery with a single leap. He slithered in the muck, kept his balance, and ran on; he had a hundred yards' start, and no one else was in sight. This man was dressed in dark clothes, so the other might still be near the drive.

A deafening roar sounded in Dawlish's ears. He started and swung round. Homer, gun in hand, was just behind him.

"Thanks," said Dawlish. He snatched the gun away, so startling Homer that the young American missed a step. Dawlish

17

veered left, towards the garage, and the drive. The man in light brown was running now, and he scrambled over the hedge separating the drive itself from the orchard. "Garage," Dawlish grunted and ran towards it.

"What the heck!" Homer cried. "This way."

Dawlish ignored him. The garage doors were open, and his massive Bentley with its sleek modern lines faced the drive. He jumped in, and the engine was turning when Homer appeared, hair awry, face flushed, lips parted.

Homer got in beside him and slammed the door, then jerked back, as Dawlish started off with a jolt. Two men came from the far side of the house as the car started down the drive—the taxi-driver and the handyman. Uncle Zeb was hurrying from the front door, and calling.

"Later," said Dawlish, and waved.

The car shot down the drive, and Homer was still trying to get his breath back. Dawlish passed the gates, jammed on the brakes, and swung right. Trees and the banks of the drive hid most of the orchard and the two men. The road ahead sloped, but the car went up in top, touching fifty by the time they reached the first sharp bend. Dawlish swung round, wings scraping the hedge. Here the road narrowed and there was barely room for two cars to pass. Two or three hundred yards ahead were the trees behind which the two-seater had been hidden.

The man in light brown had reached the road by the trees and was springing ahead of them. As they turned a bend, they saw his companion, already at the wheel of the two-seater.

Homer leaned forward and took his automatic from the dashboard pocket. Before he fired, the man in light brown had reached the little car and was clambering over the side, as his companion reversed with furious energy. The engine roared.

They were still a hundred yards away when it started along the road, like a bullet from the gun.

Homer, leaning out of the window, fired twice; the reports didn't sound so loud. Neither bullet hit the little car, but it hadn't the speed of the Bentley and was now only fifty yards away.

"All right," Dawlish said. "We'll get them."

As he spoke, the man in light brown turned round in the little car; they didn't see his gun, but he was pointing at them. Two spurts of flame followed, two muffled roars—and then a deafening report. The Bentley swerved across the road, the wheel jolted out of Dawlish's hands. He grabbed it again. The car scraped a tree, spun round, and came to a standstill broadside across the road.

Without speaking, Homer flung open the door, jumped out, and ran along the road. The roaring beat of the smaller car's engine was already fading. Dawlish lit a cigarette and began to smile; he was sitting and smiling when Homer reappeared, flushed and brushing back his hair. He still carried the gun, and as he drew nearer, thrust it into a shoulder holster.

"Not a hope," he said.

"I know you're fast, but not as fast as that," said Dawlish, and held out his hand. "Thanks."

"For what?"

"Your piece of hardware."

"Now, listen—"

"Give," said Dawlish, still holding out his hand. "I have a certain responsibility for Felicity's cousin, and I don't want to see you in gaol within a few hours of reaching this country."

Homer scowled, dug his hand inside his coat, and passed over the gun. Dawlish's right hand dwarfed it.

"That's fine," he said. "Ever changed a wheel on an automobile?"

"I suppose that's my chore," Homer said grudgingly. He went

round to the back, and Dawlish joined him as he opened the luggage compartment.

"There's an automatic jack. It won't take long," he said, and started to unstrap the spare wheel. They pulled it out, but before they had trundled it to the front of the car the engine of another sounded. Dawlish rested the wheel against the wing, and turned to see the Daimler, with Uncle Zeb sitting next to the driver, and the Four Ways' handyman at the back.

The Daimler stopped a few yards away.

"You all right?" Uncle Zeb called, and came hurrying. "No one hurt?"

"Not even the bad men," said Dawlish.

"I'd rather they escaped than either of you got hurt," said Uncle Zeb. He sized the situation up at a glance, and then turned to the chauffeur and the handyman. "You might be good enough to change that wheel for Mr. Dawlish, and we'll return to the house in the hired car."

"Good thought," said Dawlish. "I'll drive."

"But—" began the chauffeur.

"I won't do anything to lose you your licence," Dawlish said. Homer spluttered.

"Licence! That's all you can think about. Licence! Why—"

"Homer," said Uncle Zeb firmly.

Dawlish chuckled.

"You'll get used to us, Homer."

They were getting into the Daimler, Homer at the back. A grin broke through Homer's scowl, and his father was smiling as Dawlish turned the Daimler. Once on the straight road, he glanced at the older American.

"How are things at home?" he inquired.

Uncle Zeb chuckled.

"Felicity was looking after your house-girl, I guess, and

telling her not to worry, and Elvira was standing and marvel-ling. Felicity sure has a way with her. By now I imagine she's pumping Elvira so fast that Elvira doesn't know what to say."

"She wouldn't tell the truth, I suppose," mused Dawlish hopefully.

"No, sir."

They reached the drive, and Dawlish turned in slowly.

"How many people know the truth?"

"Homer and I. Elvira knows most of it, but not all. It was Elvira who insisted on our coming straight to you."

"She doesn't carry hardware, I hope."

"She does not."

"That's fine," said Dawlish. "Well, Felicity will want to know everything, so we may as well save the story until we're all together. I don't know that we can keep this from the police, Uncle Zeb, because—"

"Just call me Zeb."

"Thanks. Because—"

"You haven't a licence to keep it to yourself," said Homer tartly.

"Now, son!"

Dawlish chuckled again; anyone hearing that would realize that he was enjoying himself. He sounded as if he were filled with deep contentment; and looked it. He pulled up outside the front door, saw Felicity and Elvira at the window of the big front room, waved, and got out.

"Ethel will take a dim view of events, and while she might promise to say nothing, she'll talk as fast as she can to the first person she sees, and that would reach the police. The Daimler hire man would expect it to be reported. He's a patient chap, but we could drive him too far. So even if it's really wise to hold it back, it can't be done. On the other hand—"

"Pat, don't stand talking out there!" called Felicity.

"On the other hand," repeated Dawlish, waving gaily, "no one in the world would be surprised at gunmen coming and raiding Four Ways. It's almost a habit. Bad men don't like me, much. I could tell the local police that a couple of gunmen appeared and were driven off and no one knows why. It doesn't have to be connected with your arrival—yet. Prefer it that way?"

"I most certainly would," Uncle Zeb said.

"All right, then," said Dawlish, and waved again to Felicity, who sprang into the hall, looking as if she were going to drag them into the house. "Hallo, sweetheart, feeling all right? I've some wonderful news for you. Uncle Zeb and the family didn't come just to see your pretty eyes, they came—"

"Pat, Ethel's almost in hysterics. She wants the police, and Elvira says—"

"She can have the police," said Dawlish, and went across to the telephone in the drawing-room. The others watched, while he waited for the Haslemere Police-station to answer. Ethel came thumping along the hall, and turned into the room like a miniature tank. She had tidied her hair, but her face was flushed, her eyes were glistening, and her hands were clenched.

"*Mister* Dawlish, I won't stay here a minute longer unless you send for the police. I just won't! Why, I might have been killed! That man turned me upside down. I shouldn't feel safe, I—"

Dawlish winked at her.

"Hallo, Haslemere Police-station? . . . Is Inspector Allen in, please? . . . Patrick Dawlish . . . Yes, I'll hold on."

"So I should think," breathed Ethel. "I was just sitting down for a minute. I've been on the go all the morning, and if anyone's earned a minute's rest, *I* have. I had my legs up on a chair, and *that's* no crime, and—and then I saw him. He had a *gun*."

22

Her eyes burned with excitement. "I started to scream. I thought my last moment had come, I did really, and he hit me across the face, and then he just put his arm under my legs *and turned me upside down*. I thought I'd broken my neck or something."

"You were wonderful, Ethel," said Dawlish solemnly. "If you hadn't warned us, anything might have happened. I expect he was after Mrs. Dawlish's jewels. I—hallo? Allen?" He turned his back on Ethel. "Yes, Dawlish here, and there's been some trouble."

He listened for a moment, and chuckled.

"Not my doing, as far as I know. You'd better come up, there may be a cartridge or two lying about. . . . No, no one's seriously hurt, but my maid had a nasty time. If it hadn't been for her courage, I don't know what would have happened. . . . Twenty minutes? Fine. Oh, you might have a look-out kept for a black two-seater coupé, number BQ213, with two men in it. . . . Fine, thanks."

"There you are, Ethel, all fixed." Dawlish put down the receiver. "I don't know whether you'll mind, but you'll probably have your picture in the papers."

Ethel's eyes rounded.

"*Really?*"

"I expect so. Of course, you don't have to tell the newspapermen just what happened. You needn't even say you were frightened. Just tell them you saw the man with the gun and shouted a warning. Think that's ethical, Homer?"

"It'll get by."

"Fine. Think you can manage in the kitchen for a bit, Ethel? Don't if you're nervous."

"Oh, *I'm* not nervous," said Ethel. "It takes more than a man with a gun to frighten *me*."

She turned and bustled off, shoulders well back, and Homer stifled a chuckle, while Elvira came forward from the window.

"Do you still want to give him to me, Felicity?"

"I'll decide later."

"Whatever you decide, I'm most certainly borrowing him," said Elvira. "Pat, what's a coupé?"

"A convertible," said Homer.

"Just the word," said Dawlish. "We've been converted from a nice, quiet, peaceful little English home into a centre of international intrigue, all in the twinkling of an eye. The police will be here in a quarter of an hour. Does that give you time to tell us what it's all about, Zeb?"

"Five minutes will be enough for that," said Zebadiah.

FOUR

SAID ZEBADIAH

Zebadiah leaned back in an easy-chair, his head resting against the back, the others grouped round him, Felicity nursing her knees as she sat on a pouffe. Elvira sat on the arm of Dawlish's chair, with a head on his shoulder. Felicity glanced at her several times, and looked quickly away. Homer had a chair to himself; being large enough for Dawlish, it dwarfed him.

"Before you can understand all this, you have to know one or two things about me," said Zebadiah. "I'm a rich man—a very rich man. I started with nothing and got married on a shoe-string, and that gave me an idea. You and Felicity don't need telling that I'm a manufacturer of boots and shoes with stores all over the United States and factories everywhere it matters. You can step into any elevator in the United States, from New York to San Francisco, and out of every twelve people with you, three will be wearing *Zeb* shoes. What you and Felicity probably don't know is that I have very little to do with my business these days. I've trustworthy executives, and I believe that if you pay good men well, you get good service.

"That's for background.

"For a mighty long time now I've been working on my hobby. I'm interested in first editions, folios, rare books of all kinds. I've a big collection, because I don't have to be cheese-paring when I buy. I've agents in most of the big cities in the world, looking out for new editions, and I buy at any price they say is a good one. Maybe I'm crazy, but I just want to get the biggest and best collection of rare books outside of a museum."

"He just dreams about books," said Elvira.

"In a way that's right," said her father. "Now it's an honest business as far as it goes, Pat. You won't need telling that there is a racket in old books. I guess there isn't a collector who hasn't bought stolen books or folios, without knowing it at the time. To protect myself against having possession of stolen books, I have all new purchases checked by the New York Police Department.

"Now you know all this," Zebadiah went on, "I can take you on to the next step. A month ago my London agent bought me a small collection. To get the good things among it, he had to buy some poor stuff; but that often happens. Among the three or four hundred books he bought were some early English hand-press books—all wonderful work, Pat, and really fine. Not valuable, but interesting. They were sent to me by air, and I had them three weeks ago. While I was examining them, actually while I was writing to Will Stenway—"

"Who is Stenway?" asked Dawlish.

"He *was* my London agent," Zebadiah said slowly. "I was writing to thank him for this find when I had a cable from his wife. He had been attacked in his shop, and murdered. Perhaps you heard about that?"

Dawlish said softly, "Yes, I heard."

"I understand that no books were stolen, but the safe was emptied," said Zebadiah. "Now I'd known Will for years. We were good friends, and when I heard what had happened to

26

him, it hurt. There wasn't much I could do. I made sure through my London lawyers that his wife was all right financially. It was a sad business, but that's all I thought about it.

"A week later, my library was raided, and some books stolen. They weren't the best books, but three of them were among those which Will Stenway had sent me in his last consignment. Homer interrupted the thieves, and they got away. They didn't take all the books they wanted, I guess, because soon afterwards I had a telephone call. I was told not to report that robbery, or there would be trouble for Elvira. At that time Elvira was up in the Adirondacks with some friends, and I was agitated some. Homer went up there to see she was all right, and there wasn't any trouble. Meanwhile I told my friends in the Police Department secretly, and they promised to keep it secret and do some work on it. They didn't get far. A week later I had another telephone call, from a man who said he was a buyer and wanted some books of mine. They were *all* the books in Stenway's last purchase for me. I told the guy to go to hell.

"Next day, Elvira was nearly killed in a hit-and-run accident. I was telephoned and warned it would happen again if I didn't sell the books. So I had the books examined by experts, and went through them myself. At first I just couldn't find any explanation of anyone's interest in them. A collector might like them, sure, but he wouldn't murder to get them. Then I found that one was phony. It had a hole in the middle, a kind of hiding-place, cut out of the pages. This was full of a white powder. I told the police, and they took the book away. That powder was marihuana.

"You following me, Pat?"

"I'm right with you," said Dawlish. "Marihuana, eh? A *very* nasty dope."

He did not appear to be greatly impressed; Homer scowled.

"That's right." Zebadiah paused. "There's one thing I haven't told you, about the man who telephoned me. He was English. Anyway, he had an English voice. The thieves Homer interrupted were American all right, but not this man. I wasn't so happy about the way the Police Department were handling the mystery. I wasn't satisfied that it could be handled back home. So I decided to come over and see what I could find out. I didn't want to leave Homer and Elvira there, and they didn't want to stay, either; they're bloodthirsty young folk. So here we are. I should add one or two little things, Pat. The New York police didn't agree with me that Elvira's accident was more than just an accident. They referred to Scotland Yard about Stenway's murder, and were told it appeared to have a simple robbery motive. They seemed to think that dope had been put in the book after it reached New York. They were mighty close about it.

"Now I could be wrong, Pat, but I think there's something in these other books Stenway bought for me. I also think there's just one place where I can find out the answer—that's in England. And I think there's just one man who could do plenty to help, and he's sitting in front of me, right now. I've Elvira's word for that."

Dawlish smiled wryly.

"He certainly has my word," said Elvira.

"Elvira, darling, you don't look comfortable there," said Felicity. "Why don't you sit in that chair?"

"Oh, I'm fine," said Elvira. "Just fine. Pat, you wouldn't refuse to help, would you? Not after we've come all this way. You couldn't."

"Couldn't I?" asked Dawlish. "That depends. Why not tell the English police about this, Zeb?"

"I don't think so much of the police. Besides, when they're

told, they'll get in touch with New York, and New York will tell them I've a bee in my bonnet. That's one reason. Another—" He shrugged, and looked at Elvira; his expression was almost blank. "Maybe you don't think she's worth it, but I don't want Elvira to be hurt. Homer can look after him self, and so can I, but—this Englishman was very emphatic about not telling the police. He discovered I'd booked my passage, and telephoned me again an hour before we left for La Guardia airport. I'm uneasy about telling the police, Pat."

"I suppose so," Dawlish rubbed the broken bridge of his nose thoughtfully. "But if the Yard learned what happened here today, they would sit up and take notice."

"That's just what I don't want, right now. If there's any publicity—"

"There needn't be. And I needn't tell the local men what it's all about. The Yard ought to know."

"Oh, *Pat*," protested Elvira.

"Elvira, darling," said Felicity. "Pat's the first to stay away from the police if he thinks it will help, but he doesn't see how it would help in this case. It's obvious that the police will be able to work best. They know all about Stenway's murder. Pat doesn't know a thing except what he read in the newspapers. Of course Pat will help, where he can. I wish it hadn't happened, but there's nothing we can do about that, is there? I must go and give Ethel a hand with luncheon. It's late already."

Elvira jumped up.

"Can I help, Felicity? I'd just love to lay the table." She hurried across and put a hand on Felicity's. "Do let me."

"Yes, of course."

When the women had gone Dawlish stretched his legs even farther, took out a cigarette-case and offered it to the others. Zebadiah refused one, and Dawlish and Homer lit up.

"There's just one other thing," said Zebadiah. "If I'd dreamed there would have been trouble here today or any day, I wouldn't have come, Pat. I didn't think that it would happen so quickly. Who would?"

"No one would." Dawlish looked lazily contented. "Agree that I tell my friend at Scotland Yard?"

"I'm glad to leave it to you."

"Thanks. Any idea why your friends came today?"

As he spoke, a car turned into the drive, and he heard the engine; the police were almost here.

Zebadiah smiled faintly.

"Maybe just to make me understand that they were serious. Maybe to try to get some books."

Dawlish sat up.

"You didn't bring them with you!"

"I brought some books, but not all of *the* books," said Zebadiah. "Most of the books this man wants are buried deep down in my bank vaults in New York, but I brought some. I thought it might be useful to have some, if I wanted to pretend to strike a bargain. Don't get me wrong, Pat. I wouldn't strike any bargain, but it's a wise thing to have a trick up one's sleeve. Don't you think so?"

"Oh, yes. Where are they?"

"In the luggage-boot of the big car, I guess. I was going to take them to my London hotel. Which reminds me, we can't stay here now. It just can't be done, whatever you and Felicity say."

"You don't know Felicity," said Dawlish. "She doesn't like to be frightened out of doing what she wants. How long are you keeping that taxi?"

"It's what you call a private-hire car," said Zebadiah. "My lawyers fixed it, and it's on hire as long as I need it—days or weeks, Pat."

"Just as long as it takes us to buy a car," said Homer.

There was a ring at the front-door bell. Dawlish smiled at Homer and went towards the door. It shouldn't be difficult to convince the Haslemere police that the attack had been against him. There was no need to bring the Americans into it yet. He had an uneasy feeling that he hadn't yet been told everything.

"Are you going to the door?" Felicity asked from the kitchen.

"Yes."

Dawlish opened the door, smiling to welcome Inspector Allen—and looked instead into the face of a stranger.

FIVE

STRANGER

"Good morning," said the stranger. "Have I the pleasure of speaking to Mr. Patrick Dawlish?"

"Yes," said Dawlish, and saw another car turn into the drive; this was Allen's.

"Then may I saw how delighted I am to meet a national figure," said the stranger warmly. He was tall, flabby and pale-faced, and had a toothy smile. He wore a Homburg hat, which he swept off his head, revealing short-cropped brown hair; he looked younger without his hat—and tougher.

He produced a card, as if by sleight of hand, and held it out.

Dawlish glanced down, and read:

Rudolph Meyer,

Old Books,
14 Court Street,

London, W.1.

Dawlish looked up into the smiling face, showed no sign

that this card had startled him, and as the police car drew up, stepped back from the door.

"Can you come back, Mr. Meyer? At half-past three, shall we say?"

"Glady, gladly!" Meyer looked at his watch. "It is now half-past one, how foolish of me to come at lunch-time. Thank you, thank you. I will be here promptly at half-past three. You are *very* kind." He beamed. "I wonder if you would add to your kindness, and tell me the best place to lunch in Haslemere?"

"Any of the big hotels," said Dawlish.

"Thank you *very* much. As I passed, I saw a shop near one of the hotels and I fancied I saw some books in the window. I may be able to mix business with pleasure."

He bowed, turned to see tall, fair-haired Allen and a Detective-Sergeant, bowed, beamed again, and went to his car. From behind, he looked a big man, and he walked very daintily.

Allen said, "Sorry I'm late, Dawlish, but—"

"Sorry I have to keep you for two minutes," said Dawlish. "You know the morning-room, don't you?" He hurried away, and Allen, who had learned never to be surprised by Patrick Dawlish, followed him into the hall and made his way to the morning-room, on the right of the passage which ran alongside the stairs.

Dawlish went into the drawing-room, and closed the door, as Homer was saying:

"I must get a pack of cigarettes out of my grip, my case is empty."

"Hurry, there's a job for you," Dawlish said. "I hope you're not hungry. There's a Mr. Rudolph Meyer, just leaving in his car. He says he's going to have lunch in Haslemere. He deals in old books. My car—"

Homer took a packet of Camels out of his pocket; it was nearly full.

"I don't remember opening a new pack," he said, and swung round, saw the open French windows, and hurried out. As he stepped out of the room, he put his hand to his coat where the gun had been, and waited just long enough to send Dawlish a reproachful glance.

"Meyer?" Zebadiah frowned. "I've heard of a Rudolph Meyer. Stenway occasionally bought from him."

"Meyer's a good salesman, so why be surprised?" said Dawlish cheerfully. "I hope not to be long with the police. Tell Felicity to start lunch without me, will you? Everyone must be famished."

"Surely. Pat—"

"Yes?"

"Whatever you advise, I'll do."

"Thanks, Zeb," said Dawlish.

Allen was standing by the morning-room window, which overlooked the rose-garden at the side of the house, and his sergeant, a burly man of middle age, was sitting on an upright chair. He jumped up as Dawlish entered.

"Oh, sit down," said Dawlish, and shook hands with Allen. "Sorry to drag you out. This would happen today, we've relatives from America, and they only arrived this morning."

Allen looked amused.

"They'll probably want to take the first passage back."

"You ought to have warned them what they were walking into," said Dawlish. "Put a paragraph in all the guide books—avoid the deceptively peaceful village of Alum, Surrey, and avoid like the plague the owner of the house of ill-fame, Four Ways."

"Now we'll stop fooling," said Allen.

"As you please. There isn't much to tell, but—"

He talked for a quarter of an hour. The sergeant made copious notes, and when the story was over, Dawlish gave Allen the freedom of the house, to go and look where he wanted, search for prints or anything which might help to find the two men. He doubted if much would be found.

He didn't go immediately into the dining-room, where he could hear the others talking, but outside, to the Daimler. The chauffeur was sitting in a deck-chair, sunning himself. He struggled up.

"Open the boot for me, will you?"

"Yes, sir."

Dawlish hardly knew what to expect, would not really have been surprised had the luggage-boot been empty. It wasn't. Inside, squeezed in without an inch to spare, was a crate of books. The single word was stencilled in black all over the crate; it was possible to see through the wooden pieces to canvas, in which the books were wrapped.

"All okay, sir?"

"Fine, thanks. Lock it again, will you? I'll get my man to help you take it upstairs. The attic. I think."

"Yes, sir."

Dawlish, whistling softly, went back into the house, washed, and joined the others at lunch.

Homer Deverall drove the Bentley as if he had been used to the car for weeks, and had no difficulty in following the big Humber which Rudolph Meyer drove. Meyer went slowly through the wide stretch of the High Street. He drew up by a large hotel outside which cars were parked, and next to which was a small antique shop. He parked his car, strolled across to the shop, studied the books in the window and slowly shook his head, then turned into the hotel. Homer was already just inside, and he entered the dining-room ahead of Rudolph Meyer.

The big room was almost empty. The waiter apologized

because most of the items on the menu were off, but recommended the cold ham and salad. Meyer sat at one window, Homer at another, and they ate leisurely. At a quarter-past three Homer paid his bill and went out, and was sitting at the wheel of his car as Meyer followed.

Meyer beamed at him.

"Lovely afternoon, isn't it? Charming spot. Beautiful weather. It makes one feel *good.*"

"Oh, sure," said Homer.

Meyer's eyes glistened.

"My dear sir, forgive me! Are you an American? Of course, of course, what a foolish question to ask! How could I fail to recognize it? Not that you have a pronounced accent, *much* less marked than many. I congratulate you on coming here. What a lovely part of England to visit! The charm of England lies in her countryside—don't you agree?"

Homer looked slightly dazed.

"Oh, sure," he said.

"I knew you would," said Meyer. "I wish I could stay and show you round a little, but I have an extremely important appointment. I hope you have a thoroughly good time in England, I do indeed. Will you have a cigarette with me?"

"Thanks a lot," said Homer.

"My dear sir, that is only a trifling return for the hospitality I have often been shown in the United States." He lit the cigarette for Homer, but did not take one himself. "We may have the pleasure of meeting again. It's a small world, a *very* small world. *Good* day."

He shook hands; Homer discovered, to his surprise, that the fingers which looked so flabby were hard, and the grip firm.

Meyer hurried to his Humber, and drove off.

Homer laughed softly and started after him, made sure that

he was heading for Alum and Four Ways, and stopped outside a telephone kiosk. As he entered it, he saw the police car on its way back. He found Dawlish's number and called him. Dawlish answered himself.

"Hallo, Homer."

"Meyer's on his way," said Homer. "He made a point of speaking to me, and I wouldn't trust him as far as I could see the back of his car."

"Homer," said Dawlish, "we have a lot in common. Hungry?"

"We had lunch in the same place."

"Then stay down in the town, and when he comes back, follow him," said Dawlish.

"Sure. But I shall feel naked."

"You'll get used to it. You needn't fear gun trouble from Mr. Meyer. He has too much to lose," said Dawlish. "I've been on the telephone to friends in London, he's in a big way of business."

"I hope you're right," said Homer.

He rang off, and went back to the car. He'd drawn up on a wide stretch of road, and the nearside wheels were on the grass. He tossed the English cigarette away, and sat at the wheel, then took out the pack and lit up a Camel, to get the taste of Meyer's out of his mouth; he did not like the taste of the unfamiliar tobacco. He needn't turn the car round yet. There was a delightful view from here over undulating, wooded country. He watched the distant movements of tractors and farm workers, yawned, and lit another cigarette.

He yawned again, and grinned.

"No wonder they call it sleepy," he said aloud, and found himself settling down more comfortably at the wheel. Dawlish would keep Meyer for at least half an hour, and there was nothing to stop him from dozing.

He tossed the stub of the second Camel away, and closed his

eyes. He was pleasantly comfortable, and really sleepy. He knew that his lips were curved upwards in a smile, as if in anticipation of some great pleasure. Gradually he fell asleep. A man who had been in a café opposite the hotel came along, picked up the stubs of the cigarettes, and put others in their place.

Homer began to dream.

It was a soft, enticing dream, of beautiful women in beautiful places. He was an actor in the dream, hero in a strange and tenuous story which had neither beginning nor end. He felt voluptuously lazy, needed to make no effort, had only to raise a hand, and beauty came to him.

He dreamt on and on.

Two or three people who walked by saw him and smiled to themselves. The expression of peaceful contentment on the sharp featured, handsome face was remarkable. He even made children smile, but he was unaware of their voices. He was also oblivious of the man who approached the car—the same man who had switched the cigarette-stubs—and, when no one else was near, spoke softly. When Homer didn't answer, the man climbed in.

Homer did not realize that he was being pushed gently from the steering-wheel, or that the other man took the wheel and started off. Not far along, the new driver, who wore gloves, turned the car and came back towards the town, but turned off right and then drove fast along the main road, in the Guildford and London direction.

A little farther along the driver went off the road among some trees, took out Homer's cigarette-case and put several of the Camels from the pack into it, and half-a-dozen from his own case. He transferred the rest of the Camels to his own pocket. Then he pulled Homer down, so that he couldn't be seen from the road, and drove off again.

Homer slept by his side, still dreaming.

The car travelled fast; the speedometer touched ninety. People stood and stared, and a cycling policeman scowled after it. Only the driver was visible. They came upon a long, straight stretch of road, and the driver slowed down until they were travelling at only fifteen miles an hour. No other traffic was in sight. The driver opened his door, turned the nose of the car towards the hedge, and jumped.

The car swung off the road and into the hedge.

SIX

RUDOLPH MEYER

No other car was in sight. The man had chosen his spot well, and luck aided him. He ran to the car, pulled Homer across the seat until he slumped down on the steering-wheel, then turned and walked in the London direction. The hedge was damaged; the nearside front wings of Dawlish's car were dented and scratched. The man, sleek and slim, hurried away as the engine of a car sounded not far off. He hid behind a tree when a high-powered car flashed by, coming from Guildford. He appeared on the road again, and a small car turned the corner and pulled up just behind him.

"All finished?" asked the driver.

"Get me away from here."

"Think you were seen?"

"Of course I wasn't seen. It's all gone well—damn well. Stop yapping."

The man who had been with Homer climbed into the seat next to the driver, who drove off at once. He had gone only a hundred yards when a stream of traffic passed in the opposite direction.

"You were lucky," he said.

"Okay, so I was lucky. You'll be lucky if you hold your job down much longer, you talk too much."

The driver shrugged, and drove on.

Near the corner the drivers of four cars noticed the Bentley, but didn't stop. A little man in a dilapidated Morris, and with a woman by his side, passed the corner, looked round, and slowed down. He waited for other cars to pass him, then swung round and went on to the grass verge.

"Is he hurt?" asked the woman anxiously.

"How do I know, May?" The little man jumped out and ran to Homer. "The car's knocked about, but he *looks* all right."

"George, what are you going to *do*?"

"Send for the police, of course," said George. "Stand out in the road and wave to the next car that comes along. Never stop, some of these people," he muttered under his breath. "Callous devils, that's what they are."

His wife was already waving at a car, and the driver pulled in. Soon he was off again, to telephone the local police.

Throughout all this Homer slept; but his dreams had gone. The sleep was more troubled.

Dawlish sat back in an easy-chair, coffee by his side, Elvira and her father sitting opposite him, Felicity in the window-seat. It was twenty-five minutes past three. Homer's telephone message had satisfied them all. The atmosphere was restful, and now and again Zebadiah's eyelids drooped; it wouldn't take much to make him fall asleep.

Dawlish caught sight of a car coming into the drive.

"Is he here?" Elvira asked eagerly.

"Yes."

"I wonder if we do know him," said Elvira. "Dad, come and see!"

She pulled her father out of his chair and led him to the window; she stood on one side and Uncle Zeb on the other, and they watched as Rudolph Meyer's car came to a standstill, near the front door.

"No, I guess I haven't seen him before," said Uncle Zeb.

"I certainly don't know him." Elvira turned away from the window. "Will you see him in here, Pat?"

"No, the morning-room. Then if all of you go into the dining-room, you'll hear practically everything we say."

"With the doors open?"

"You can close the doors."

Dawlish stood up, as the bell rang. Elvira frowned as he disappeared, then turned to ask Felicity what he meant.

"He loves to be mysterious," said Felicity lightly. "There's a kind of ventilation slot running round the walling between the morning-room and the drawing-room—he had it built that way, because—"

"Things like this are *always* happening? You mean, he prepared for it?"

"I mean he was always prepared for it," said Felicity.

They heard Dawlish talking to Rudolph Meyer; heard the two men leave the hall and go into the morning-room; the door closed, firmly, and the voices were cut off. Elvira led the way across to the dining-room, excited but moving very quietly. Her father followed, smiling faintly. He put a hand on Felicity's arm.

"It must be difficult living with your husband."

"It is," said Felicity, ruefully. "You might tell him so, he never seems to believe me."

Uncle Zeb squeezed her arm.

"I'll listen for a while, then use your telephone, if I may."

"Of course."

In the morning-room, with its bright chintzes, its flowers,

and its charm, Mr. Rudolph Meyer was standing and looking round, admiring everything he saw.

"Now," said Meyer, "if I may came to the point of my journey—my eager desire to have your advice, possibly even your *help*, Mr. Dawlish. I recently sold some books to a London dealer, a reputable man. I am implying nothing against the dead, but—"

"Who is dead?"

"The man to whom I sold these books. I say recently. I mean a month ago. He died, unfortunately, of violence. He was—"

"Murdered," said Dawlish, sepulchrally.

Mr. Meyer closed his eyes and folded his hands across his stomach.

"He was *murdered*," he echoed. "I knew him well. He was a scrupulously fair man, and no doubt was murdered for gain. Money and valuables were stolen from his shop, but I think it possible that *books* were also stolen. That has never been reported. I am happy to have the confidence of some of the officers at Scotland Yard, and I have it on unshakable evidence that no loss of books was reported when poor Stenway died. Poor Stenway."

"Ah, yes," said Dawlish.

"Now believe it or not," said Meyer, "I believe that the books which I sold to Stenway were stolen. There can be no certainty, at this stage, but I am very anxious to find out. The man from whom I bought the books is a valued client, and he now wishes he had not sold the books. I won't go into details, but confidentially I can tell you that he sold them because he was a little hard-up, but has since recouped certain losses and would like those books back. I endeavoured to get them from Stenway's shop—his assistant is now running it for his poor, bereaved wife. He couldn't trace the books or any record of their sale. There *is* a record of the purchase from me.

"Now, Mr. Dawlish, I want those books back. My client is prepared to pay substantially for them. However, I have worked through all the usual channels, including my good friends at Scotland Yard, and they are unable to help me. So—I come to you."

He paused, whipped out a yellow pigskin wallet, flipped it open, and took out a cheque. He thrust this forward into Dawlish's hand, and breathed:

"Here is a *blank* cheque. That is a measure of my confidence in you. *Will* you help, Mr. Dawlish?"

Dawlish examined the cheque with interest. It was small and pale blue in colour; Mr. Rudolph Meyer had a large signature, and liked purple ink.

Dawlish flipped the slip of paper with his thumb.

"Who is your client?"

"I cannot disclose that, Mr. Dawlish. It is a highly confidential matter. But dealing with me is practically the same as dealing with a principal, I assure you. I—"

"Sorry," said Dawlish, and was almost brusque. "No name, no deal."

He held the cheque out.

"But I can't understand you," said Meyer. "The case interests you. It is a pretty little mystery, and yet—"

The telephone bell rang, and the instrument was at Dawlish's elbow.

"Excuse me," he said, and lifted the receiver.

SEVEN

P.C. BOWDY

There was another instrument in the next room, and Felicity was probably already at that; a third extension was upstairs in the bedroom.

"Mr. Dawlish," a man said, in a deep voice. "Are you the owner of a Bentley, registration number BX 2110?"

"Yes."

"Thank you, sir. I am a police officer of Birley Village. Can you inform me of the whereabouts of your car?"

It should have been waiting near Haslemere, with Homer at the wheel.

"I lent it to a friend. I don't know where he's taken it."

"Would you be good enough to describe this friend?"

"Short, dark, dressed in pale blue, American. Is he hurt?"

"He's not *hurt*, sir, so far as I can find out, but the car is damaged. Not seriously, I'm glad to say." The constable suddenly became human. "Tell you the truth, Mr. Dawlish, I thought it was your car. I've been trying to get you for some minutes, but your line was engaged. It's your friend all right, but you shouldn't have let him out with it, not in his condition. The doctor says he's not fit to be at the wheel, he—"

"Drunk?" asked Dawlish, incredulously.

"Not drunk, sir. *Drugged.*"

Dawlish said, "Oh, no!"

"Sorry, sir. Yes."

"Where is he now?"

"At my cottage, sir. I had him brought along. The doctor's here with him, now. He's coming out of his stupor. Care to come along and have a word with me, Mr. Dawlish?"

"You're very good," said Dawlish. "I'll be along right away. Birley Village?"

"That's right, sir. Last house in on the far side along the main road."

"Thanks," said Dawlish. "I'll be seeing you."

He put back the receiver.

Meyer murmured, "Mr. Dawlish, if you would reconsider—"

"Sorry." Dawlish beamed at him. "Principals only. You'll excuse me, won't you. A friend has been involved in a slight accident, I must go and help him."

"Really? I'm so sorry. Please don't trouble to show me out. Thank you for your consideration, for giving me so much time. You have my card, and if you *should* decide to change your mind, do let me know."

He rose, turned, and hurried along the hall, and Dawlish did not follow him. He opened the front door and went out, without glancing round. As the door slammed, and Dawlish saw his face with that bleak look in his eyes as if it were still in the hall, the dining-room door opened and Elvira rushed out.

"Pat! What's happened to Homer? What's happened?"

Uncle Zeb was in the doorway.

"Nothing serious, I gather," said Dawlish. He glanced at Felicity, who was just by her uncle's side. His eyes asked the question: have you told them about the drug? Felicity shook her head. "We'll use your hired car, Zeb. The chauffeur won't mind, I hope."

Elvira rushed to the door.

"Will you wait—" Dawlish began, to Felicity.

"No," said Felicity.

Dawlish grinned. "Very well, dear."

Uncle Zeb said softly, "Pat, I can't expect you to think as much of Homer as I do, but it's serious to me."

"Nothing to worry about so far as the accident's concerned," Dawlish said. "It looks as if I'll have to bail Homer out, that's all."

Felicity had gone upstairs for a coat and handbag, but she was down again as Dawlish started the engine of the car. Uncle Zeb sat next to him, and the women behind. In the distance they saw Rudolph Meyer's car disappearing towards Haslemere. At the foot of the drive Dawlish turned right, and Elvira said:

"It's the other way, surely."

"Short cut," said Dawlish.

"Be quiet, Elvira." Uncle Zeb's tone suggested that his word was law and she must obey. "Pat, that man told you a remarkable story. If it were true, then he sold the books to Stenway, and someone wants them pretty badly."

"Didn't we know?"

"I mean, someone else."

"Do you?" asked Dawlish.

Elvira burst out, "If there's a man I don't like, it's a man who speaks in riddles! Patrick, what do *you* mean?"

"That Meyer is probably working for the man who's been working on you, and is trying to distract us," said Dawlish, driving fast along the narrow road which led towards the open land of Surrey.

"Let me get this clear," said Uncle Zeb.

"It *is* clear," declared Felicity promptly. "Pat thinks that Meyer is behind it, that he soon discovered that you had come here, and he was afraid of what might happen if he started working for you, and caused a distraction. To confuse the issue—put up a red herring, if you like. And it's clever too—isn't it, Pat?"

"So-so," said Dawlish.

"*What's* clever?" asked Elvira tensely.

"Meyer has hinted that he's been trying to get these books honestly; that he doesn't know where they are; that he doesn't know they were sent to America and therefore he doesn't know anything about what's been happening to you. Isn't that right, Pat?"

"It could be."

"Would he come to you, if he were guilty?" asked Uncle Zeb.

"He might," said Dawlish. "I did not take to Rudolph Meyer. Homer had a pleasant little chat with him, too—he told us so over the telephone. Following that, Homer goes dashing off with the car, and—"

"It's not like Homer."

"What isn't?"

"He was to watch this man Meyer, at your request, and if Homer starts a job, it takes plenty to make him let go."

"He *wouldn't* let go," said Elvira. "He's too good."

"He did," murmured Felicity.

"But—"

"How long has Homer been taking drugs?" asked Dawlish.

He regretted only one thing; that he couldn't look into Uncle Zeb's eyes as he put the question. He heard Elvira take in a sharp breath, and, glancing round, saw Uncle Zeb start and turn his head; Uncle Zeb looked dumbfounded. He was badly shaken; was it simply by surprise or astonishment, or had he some idea that his son was a dopy?

"*Homer* take *drugs?*" breathed Elvira. "Why, that's just silly.

That's absurd. *Homer*? Why, only last year he did a big job tracking down a marihuana ring, for the F.B.I. Homer just hates the thought of drugs."

Uncle Zeb said, "That's true. Homer is with the Federal Bureau of Investigation. You're wrong, Pat. I don't know who told you about this dope, but it's not true. I'll stake my life on it."

Dawlish stepped into the parlour of the policeman's cottage, and smiled at the tall figure of Dr. Eric Scott, from Haslemere, who was standing by the window. Scott was young, fresh-faced, and an old friend; he owed much to Patrick Dawlish.

They shook hands.

"What's all this, Eric? Where's the patient?"

"In the next room. The policeman's wife is looking after him. He'll be all right."

"Sure about drugs?"

"Oh, yes, not a shadow of doubt," said Scott. "I saw a lot of this one, when I was in the Far East. He's had a fairly strong dose of hashish—"

"Marihuana?"

"More or less the same thing, grown in a different place. I thought it might be wise to take him to hospital, but Bowdy was anxious to have him here; he doesn't often get anything unusual, and provided I could watch him I knew he'd be all right. It all measures up, too. Bowdy was on the road when he drove past at a crazy speed, as if he were drunk. It would quite likely affect him that way. Then he would go off into a nice, pretty dream, and later start working out of it. He's pretty well worked out now, but I shouldn't question him much yet. He looks weak."

"Well, well," said Dawlish. "You'd say there's no shadow of doubt."

"Now look here, I'm talking as a friend," said Scott. "I wouldn't swear to it in a court—I would just say that he had all the symptoms. I don't know anything else that gives the same symptoms. I could probably use a stomach pump and make absolutely sure, but—"

"No, I don't think we'll need that," said Dawlish. "Pity you told the constable."

"Yes, I was afraid so. He was talking about drink, and I said I wasn't so sure, it might be a drug. He was on it like a shot, and I either had to lie to the chap or tell him what I thought. Bowdy's no fool."

"Well, thanks, Eric. When can he be moved?"

"Any time, if he's kept warm."

"Thanks again," said Dawlish. "Would this come if he'd just had one dose? Or does it mean addiction?"

"I'm a doctor, not a crystal-gazer! I shouldn't think it necessarily meant addiction."

"Meaning it could be," said Dawlish. "I'll be seeing you, Eric!"

He went out into the tiny hall, and found the others waiting in a small room opposite. With them was Police-constable Bowdy. Elvira insisted on going in to see Homer, and Uncle Zeb followed her; the bustling wife of the policeman went with them. Dawlish caught a glimpse of Homer, lying flat on the bed, his face nearly as pale as the pillow-cases.

"Excuse me, Mr. Dawlish." Bowdy laid fingers like sausages on Dawlish's arm. "Come with me a minute, will you?" He led the way back into the sitting-room where he had his desk. "I'm worried about this, Mr. Dawlish, and I would be even if it wasn't a friend of yours. Look at these."

He took a cigarette-case out of his pocket; the monogram on the gold was *H.D.* He opened it, and six cigarettes, all plump and pale brown in colour, not white like the Camels beside them, fitted snugly inside.

"No name on them, sir, and I can't *smell* anything funny, but they're not ordinary cigarettes. The case was poking out of his pocket, so I put it in mine to make sure he didn't lose it."

"Very wise," said Dawlish.

Yet Homer had said his case was empty.

"Thank you, sir. It's a funny thing anyhow. I *saw* that car, doing at least ninety and swaying right across the road. Passed me like the wind, he did, and—it's a *very* funny thing. The young American gentleman's hair couldn't be any blacker, could it?"

Dawlish said softly, "No, it couldn't."

"Funny how you notice things," mused Bowdy. "I could have sworn the driver of that car wasn't so dark as *he* is. He was dark, mind you. But his hair was flopping about in the wind, I could see it. The American lad's hair is plastered down. Doesn't look as if it's been disturbed at all. And I just don't think the driver's looked as dark as all that; I don't really. Peculiar, isn't it?"

"Bowdy," said Dawlish warmly, "you ought to be in the detective branch. It certainly is peculiar. Oh—did you find any more cigarettes in the man's pockets? A packet of Camels, nearly full?"

"No, sir, no others."

"A neat job," Dawlish said. "Yours and the crook's. Report to Inspector Allen right away, will you? Tell him everything—and also tell him I'm on my way to London to see Trivett of Scotland Yard."

"*Very* good, sir." Bowdy's eyes glistened. "Mr. Dawlish, I wonder if—"

He broke off.

"Anything, old chap."

"Me and my missus, we've often said we'd like to live in London," said Bowdy. "There's a chance for a man there, and I'm quite young, as young goes in the Force. Thirty-seven. If ever you got a chance to put a word in, it's amazing what a man like Mr. Trivett could do, if he tried. You don't mind my asking, do you?"

"It'll be the first thing I do," promised Dawlish.

EIGHT

SCOTLAND YARD

"Hello, Bill," said Dawlish, as he entered the office of Superintendent William Trivett of New Scotland Yard. "If you want a really smart recruit, with none of your London Robert's sophistication, I've just the man for you. Powers of observation that would shatter most of your detective officers, and his only drawback a face like a disheartened bull. Interested?"

"No," said Trivett, and shook hands warmly. "I'm never interested in anyone you recommend. He'd be either unreliable or unsafe."

"Poor Bowdy," said Dawlish, and dropped into an arm-chair which Trivett indicated.

"I gather you've had an American invasion," Trivett went on.

"Nicely put. Felicity's relatives—she isn't sure whether to be mad with them or mad with me because I haven't been quick enough."

Trivett picked up a manilla folder.

"I think I've everything here. The men who attacked you at Four Ways. You tried to fob off Allen, but he had a suspicion that it was to do with the American visitors. One of the visitors is your cousin—is it a cousin?"

"Felicity's."

"For better or worse, remember," Trivett said. "*Your* Cousin Homer was in trouble. Where is he?"

"At home, being nursed by Elvira, his sister, and Felicity. Allen kindly put a man at the drive gates, to try to frighten off anyone else who showed an interest. I called Tim Jeremy just before I left, and he's on the way down, to make sure he doesn't miss any fun."

"Your uncle?"

"Uncle Zeb's here. Downstairs."

"I've had a word with Merryweather of *The Cry* about him," said Trivett. "Zebadiah Deverall, multi-millionaire owner of Zeb shoes, collector of rare folios and first editions. Nothing else known against him! No scandal, as far as Merry knows, and if there had been, he would know. What's his worry?"

Dawlish contemplated the ceiling for a minute, then told the story exactly as it had been told to him. He added the incident of the attack and the fact that Homer had gone to keep an eye on a mysterious caller; but he did not, at that stage, name the caller.

"That's where Bowdy comes in. He happened to be cycling along the road when my car passed at ninety something. He caught just a glimpse. Later, he found Homer, at the wheel, dead to the world. Any way of checking whether Homer is F.B.I., by the way?"

"I can try. They often won't tell."

"Try hard, won't you? Well, Homer has dark hair—raven's-wing stuff and plenty of it, and heavily oiled; there wasn't a hair out of place. Bowdy says the driver's hair was blowing about in the wind that cut in through the window, and anyhow, he wasn't as dark as that. Not bad, you'll agree."

"Who's Bowdy?"

"Country copper with London ambitions."

"You tell him to be a wise man and stay in the country," said Trivett. "It was quick, I'll grant you. What else did he do?"

"He saved Homer's cigarette-case from falling out of his pocket," Dawlish said with a lazy grin, and put a hand to his own pocket. "I think he saw me take this out of the case, too, but turned a blind eye." He handed Trivett a white envelope, in which was one of the brown cigarettes. "He thinks that's unusual and that it might be the source of the dope."

Trivett fingered it cautiously at one end and sniffed.

"Do you?"

"What's the Yard laboratory for?"

Trivett pressed a bell, and spoke while he waited for a sergeant to come in.

"Where are the other cigarettes?"

"Allen has them, I think."

The door opened at a tap, and a spruce young man came in.

"Yes, sir?"

"Take this up to the lab and ask for a report right away, Gregg," said Trivett, handing over the cigarette, still in its envelope. "Bring the report yourself—you'd better wait while they do it, or they'll put it aside and forget all about it."

"Right, sir!" Gregg went out briskly.

Trivett returned to Dawlish's story.

"I remember the Stenway murder, of course, although I didn't handle it myself. It seemed all right, straightforward robbery— money, not books. I suppose Felicity's millionaire uncle isn't out for notoriety?"

"I think he's in trouble and has come over here to get out of it."

"And you also think that the people who are after the books were on his tail from the moment he reached London, and were jittery when he came straight down to see you. With your usual modesty!"

"That's right."

"Who was Homer watching?"

"Rudolph Meyer," said Dawlish simply.

Trivett's expression changed. He opened a drawer in his desk, took out an envelope, extracted a photograph, and held it out.

"That Rudolph?"

Dawlish nodded.

"Well," said Trivett, "I don't know what to make of Rudolph Meyer. He's probably the greatest expert on old books in the country. We've consulted him a number of times, and he's never been wrong. He tumbles over himself to please—not only us, but everyone he comes in contact with. He gives a fortune away to charity, seems to make a fortune once a week on the Stock Exchange, and—I don't trust him."

"Wise man."

"I don't know," said Trivett, looking at the photograph. "He's never been suspected even remotely of any funny business. In the trade no one likes him and everyone trusts him. His word's his bond, that kind of boast, and he lives up to it. He has a pretty young wife, and appears to idolize her. He'll go to fantastic lengths to get what his clients want, and he has a list of clients as long as your arm—all wildly wealthy. It's rumoured that he gets his 'Change tips from them. He certainly gets them from somewhere. He has a villa at Mentone, a chalet in Switzerland, an estate in the Bahamas, and clients all over the world. I still don't trust him, but he wouldn't do anything so crazy as get mixed up in crime this way. He might be at the back of it, pulling strings, but he wouldn't come right out into the open."

"Wouldn't he?" murmured Dawlish.

"I shouldn't expect him to. Pat—" Trivett leaned forward, still playing with the photograph. "Do you seriously suggest that Homer Deverall was watching Meyer, that Meyer wanted to shake him off, drugged him and sent him off in your car with another man, who left him and made it look as if he's been driving?"

"Yes."

"Not Rudolph Meyer," said Trivett emphatically.

Dawlish shrugged.

"Now if someone were trying to frame Meyer, they might try it that way. It's far too obvious for Meyer himself. I can't see him taking any risk with his reputation. He's too proud of it. What did he want with you?"

Dawlish told him.

Trivett said slowly, "He certainly inquired about a number of books which he said he'd sold to Stenway, and which he couldn't trace. He also said that he thought they must have been stolen, as there was no record at Stenway's shop. Stenway's assistant, Oliver, who's keeping things going, was certain of that."

"Supposing we have Deverall up, and see what you think of him? I've told him that I'm going to tell you everything, in confidence, and that after the Homer incident it won't be possible to work without the police knowing."

"Even you have gleams of common sense." Trivett lifted the telephone and spoke to the sergeant in charge of the waiting-room. "Jones, send Mr. Deverall up to my office, will you? He—"

Trivett broke off.

Dawlish leaned forward abruptly in his chair.

"Oh, I see," said Trivett. "Thanks. Let me know if he comes back, will you?"

Trivett said slowly, "Odd friends you have, Pat. Relations, I mean. Ten minutes after you'd left him, he had a message. A boy brought it. The sergeant took it from the boy and handed it to Deverall, who read it, got up, and went off, saying that he'd be back in a few minutes. That was twenty minutes ago."

Trivett stopped; and there was a long silence, before Dawlish said softly:

"Well, well. Call Four Ways, Bill. Make sure everything's all right there, will you?"

NINE

WALK OUT

Trivett put the call in to Four Ways, replaced the receiver to wait for it to come through, frowned, and pressed the tips of his fingers together.

"Now look here, Pat, there's no need to get alarmed. Just because Deverall walked out, that doesn't mean there's any trouble at Haslemere."

"No," said Dawlish.

"Deverall may—" began Trivett, and stopped.

"That's right." Dawlish got up slowly. "There's no sensible explanation of Deverall walking out. It's not the kind of thing I should have expected from Uncle Zeb. Who sent him the letter? Why did it make him get up and walk? We weren't followed on the road. I kept a careful watch when we reached Kingston, to make sure we weren't picked up on the by-pass. If we were followed, it was after we reached London, and how could anyone pick us out of the traffic here?"

Trivett shrugged. "You could be making too much of it."

"Oh, yes," said Dawlish. He stood by the window, massive and unmoving, and his voice sounded flat. "I could be. But what are the facts? Someone knows that Uncle Zeb came here. Uncle Zeb wasn't followed, so the Yard must have been watched. As soon as we'd come in, the watcher sent the letter. I wonder what Zeb would have done had I been with him when he read it? I fancy he would still have walked out. It would take something pretty big to make him leave here now. Don't you people ever get telephone calls in a hurry?"

"It'll be through in a minute," said Trivett. He lifted another receiver. "Hurry that call to Alum, please, and give me the duty sergeant in the hall. I'll hold on."

Dawlish lit another cigarette.

"Hallo, Sergeant," said Trivett briskly. "You were in the hall when Mr. Dawlish and Mr. Deverall came in, weren't you?"

"Yes, sir."

"See anyone at the gates, or in the street, who seemed interested in them?"

"Can't say I did, sir, but I'll ask Clarke. He was on the gate when they arrived. He's just been relieved. Will you hold on, sir?"

"Yes."

The other telephone bell rang, and Trivett motioned to the instrument as Dawlish moved from the window.

"Hallo," said Dawlish, in a quiet voice.

Felicity said, "Pat!"

It might have been imagination, but he thought that there was anxiety in her voice; she wasn't just ordinarily glad to hear him.

"Pat, Elvira's really worried. Have you any news?"

Dawlish listened for several minutes, was mildly reassuring, and replaced the receiver; his expression was blank, almost foolish. Trivett had also finished his conversation.

Dawlish grinned. "All's well at Four Ways. What about your duty sergeant?"

"Nothing. The constable at the gates didn't notice anyone lounging about opposite—you came in the Embankment gate, didn't you? No one was in sight on the Embankment, but that doesn't mean that someone wasn't hanging around. The boy who brought the message was about fifteen, office-boy type, and the duty sergeant thought nothing of it."

"No reason why he should."

"Nothing wrong at Four Ways, you say?"

"No. Elvira's worried, but Homer's better. Felicity would be jittery, but Tim Jeremy arrived there ten minutes ago, so she isn't alone. Bill, we've a man-sized mystery on our hands. Someone can make a phone call and write a note, and Uncle Zeb just does what he tells him. No word of explanation, nothing." His voice took on a harsh note. "Send a call out, Bill. There's reason to believe Zeb may be in danger; you've evidence of that."

Trivett swung round to his desk.

"Confound it, I can't send a call out. He can't possibly be called missing. I can't warn the London and Home Counties police forces to keep a look-out for someone who will probably turn up in half an hour's time."

"You'll regret it, Bill," Dawlish said.

He moved towards the door, but before he reached it, it opened and Gregg came hurrying in.

"Here's the report, sir. Marihuana. West Indian or American probably. The Chief Chemist is quite sure of it, sir. And there's a pretty strong dose in the cigarette."

Trivett took the envelope, in which the cigarette was now a sorry-looking mess of torn paper and shredded tobacco. He wasn't happy.

"Oh, don't worry about a trifle like that," said Dawlish brightly. "It's only in a few cigarettes which have been handed out to visiting Americans. Who cares about a little dream-drug?"

Gregg, startled, glanced from one man to the other.

The telephone bell rang.

"Answer that, Gregg," said Trivett, and rounded his desk and approached Dawlish. "Pat, be sensible over this. I don't like it, but if I started the inquiry and your relations turned up unharmed, I'd be on the carpet for wasting both public funds and the time of my men—they've plenty to do already. And the A.C. would—"

"It's from Haslemere, sir," said Gregg.

Trivett swung round and went across to his desk. He didn't sit down, but listened, made a few non-committal grunts, and finally said:

"Thanks very much, Allen, I'll keep in touch."

He rang off, and stood by the corner of the desk. He didn't speak for a moment, but rubbed the side of his nose. Gregg glanced at him, expecting instructions, and began to feel embarrassed; that there was a clash between Dawlish and Trivett was obvious.

"Want me any more, sir?"

"Not now, Gregg, thanks."

Gregg went out without another word.

"What is it?" Dawlish demanded gruffly.

"I think you were right about one thing," said Trivett in a curiously low-pitched voice. "This P.C. Bowdy is pretty good. In his off-duty hours he poked around a bit, discovered that your Bentley with Homer at the wheel was parked just outside Haslemere this afternoon, and had a look round the spot. He found the stub of a cigarette, like those found in Homer Deverall's case, and two Camel stubs."

Trivett paused; Dawlish didn't interrupt him.

"The first was almost certainly loaded with the drug," Trivett went on. "Bowdy has been studying finger-prints for a long time, and does some experimenting with a camera. He didn't ask permission, but photographed prints on that cigarette-case—Homer's. Homer's finger-prints are on the end of the cigarette which was found near the car."

"Ah," said Dawlish.

"I can understand why you want to put a word in for Bowdy." Trivett smiled rather thinly. "He's confirmed practically every-thing you suggested about Rudolph Meyer. He checked that Meyer was in the dining-room with Homer, that they spoke to each other outside, and that Meyer gave Homer a cigarette. But even Bowdy can't be sure that the stub came from the cigarette which Meyer handed out."

"Oh, no," said Dawlish. "And we can't allow such a thing as circumstantial evidence, can we?"

"We can keep all this in mind," said Trivett, "and it may come in useful later. I tell you that Meyer may be a bad egg, but wouldn't risk losing his reputation, not to mention his freedom, by coming out into the open. If we're ever going to catch Meyer out, it will have to be done subtly."

"Ah," said Dawlish again. "Going to put that call out for Uncle Zeb?"

"No, I am not. Don't read too much into this business, Pat. Wait until morning, and your uncle may turn up."

TEN

DAWLISH INQUIRES

At nearly half-past seven Dawlish drew up outside the American Embassy in Grosvenor Square, glanced at the statue of Roosevelt opposite the front door, strolled into the hall, and was greeted by a firm but affable doorman. Dawlish asked for Mr. Vernon C. Harding, and was told that Mr. Harding was engaged. He scribbled the word "urgent" on a card and had it taken in.

Soon a tall, fresh-looking girl came hurrying to him.

"I'm sorry to have kept you waiting, Mr. Dawlish. Mr. Harding can see you right away."

She led the way to a lift; they went up two floors, walked a short distance along a wide passage, and stopped at a door marked: "Vernon C. Harding." The girl opened it, and Dawlish stepped into the room, as a young man rose from a chair behind a mammoth desk. The door closed. Harding held out his hand and smiled.

"I'm very glad to see you again, Dawlish," he said. "Sit down, please. What's urgent?"

"If you were to ask Scotland Yard they would tell you that I'm making up part of it," said Dawlish. "I'm worried about an

American citizen. He's been missing for about one hour. He was shot at this afternoon, within a few hours of arriving in England. Efforts have been made to frame his son on a drug charge—it won't succeed, but it was a good try. So I'm worried."

"Who's this family?"

"Zeb shoes."

"Is that so?" Harding was impressed. "Old Zeb himself? I heard he was coming over. That's bad, Dawlish. Shot at? Son framed? Missing? Why doesn't the Yard think it's serious?"

"He went out willingly, apparently."

"I see their point," murmured Harding. "What do you want me to do?"

Dawlish smiled amiably.

"You can work miracles," he said. "I'd like you to have a word with your Ambassador, and ask him to telephone the Home Secretary in person. Zeb Deverall's been in trouble with gangsters on the other side, so would Scotland Yard give him special protection? As a favour, from the Home Secretary to the American Ambassador! After that, Scotland Yard would do everything anyone ever asked them to do about Zeb."

Harding's eyes were gleaming.

"Was Zeb in trouble back home?"

"Yes. Threats. He came here because they started from here, but you needn't tell the Ambassador that, unless you want to. I'm really worried about Zeb."

"Well," said Harding, "I'll see what I can do. The Ambassador may want to know more."

"You can convince him," Dawlish murmured.

Harding chuckled, and went out.

He was gone for twenty minutes.

"All fixed," he said as he came in.

"Nice work," said Dawlish.

"The luck was with you. The Ambassador knows Zeb," said Harding. "He's leaving for a social date right now, or he would want to see you. Anything more I can do?"

"Check Homer and Elvira Deverall's behaviour at home."

"Sure."

"Thanks," said Dawlish. He exchanged another powerful handshake, and went out. The tall, bright-faced, and nice-looking secretary took him downstairs and wished him good-bye. He went down the steps on to the pavement as a car started to move off on his right.

He heard a sharp report and saw a flash from the grass in front of the Roosevelt statue; or rather, from a gun in the hand of a man standing on the grass. He heard the whang as a bullet hit the roof of the car. He knew, in that swift second of thought, that the car had started off at the one moment which saved him from being wounded; had perhaps saved his life. He could see over the top of the car, and a man was running; no one was after him, but several people walking across the square stared at the man.

He was smallish, dressed in light brown, and he ran swiftly; Dawlish had seen him on the banks of the drive at Four Ways.

Dawlish leapt into the roadway behind the car, and raced towards the square, fifty yards behind the man in the light-brown suit.

He didn't have a chance to catch the sharpshooter. The man reached a small car, a four-seater and not a coupé, on one side of the square, and was driving off before Dawlish had reduced the gap from fifty to thirty yards. The man didn't shoot again. Two or three people stared at him, but none made the slightest attempt to stop him.

The car disappeared. Over by the Embassy, a policeman stood by the car which had been hit by the bullet.

* * *

Dawlish walked until he found a telephone kiosk, and stepped inside.

He telephoned a Flaxman number, and a woman answered him brightly.

"Hallo?"

"Joan, my sweet, you sound as beautiful as ever."

"Who—oh, *Pat*, you fool!"

"But I meant it," protested Dawlish.

"Not a hope," said Joan Beresford. "Where are you? Can you come over—Ted will be back by ten, he'd be delighted to find you waiting for him."

"I'll try to look in, but I may have to get back tonight. I'll ring Ted again, anyhow. I'll be seeing you—tell Ted I rang."

"Yes, of course."

Dawlish stepped out of the kiosk, and glanced up and down the street. Twenty or thirty people were in sight, all of them walking briskly, none showing any interest in him. He went back to Grosvenor Square, approaching from a different direction, aiming for his car. No one appeared to notice him, there were no crowds. Dawlish reached his car and drove off.

A few minutes later he decided that he ought to have called Trivett, after all. He drove on, slowly, thoughtfully. From the moment he had been shot at the complexion of the case had changed; became deadly.

He thought of Joan Beresford.

Ted, her husband, was his closest friend, not second even to Timothy Jeremy, who was now at Four Ways. The three men had worked together often. Of late Ted, who years ago had lost a leg in the course of a case, had worked less than Tim—because of Joan and his children.

He decided that it was a good thing Ted had been out, as he

drove towards Charing Cross Road. In a narrow street, called Niven Row, were a dozen shops; eight of them bookshops. At the far end of the street was a telephone kiosk.

It was nearly dark; lights were on, in windows and on cars. He went to the kiosk, put in his pennies, and dialled Scotland Yard, for the call he ought to have made. Trivett was still in his office.

"Bill?"

"Hallo, Pat," said Trivett. Nothing in his voice indicated that he had received special instructions about Deverall. "I thought you'd soon be back."

"Is Uncle Zeb?"

"No."

"Remember what I told you," said Dawlish, and rang off.

He stayed in the kiosk, and watched the third shop along on the road. In one of the others there was a light in the shop itself; the only light in the third building was from a window on the first floor, and it spread a yellow glow about the narrow street and the shops opposite. Shadows moved.

Stenway's was the shop with the light on at the first floor. Stenway's assistant, Charles Oliver, lived above the shop premises, as he had during Stenway's lifetime.

Dawlish waited for half an hour, and wondered if he were being over-cautious.

He had seen no one of interest go in or out of the Row. The light was still on in the room above the shop, but he didn't see any shadows now. He went along, and rang the bell at the door beside the shop.

There was no answer.

He rang again, expecting to hear footsteps; but they didn't come. The light above burned steadily.

He looked down at the lock of the door; a Yale lock. He

hesitated, and then took a small key-case out of his pocket; it also had a pocket. Out of this he took a strip of mica, three inches long, one wide; the commonest use for a piece of mica of that size was to force Yale locks. No one turned into the Row. He pushed the mica in; when it was in the right position, the lock would click back.

ELEVEN

STENWAY'S SHOP

One more push, and he heard the lock click back; he opened the door without trouble, so it wasn't bolted.

Light shone from the landing at the top of a flight of stairs—narrow, carpeted stairs, and the carpet was threadbare. A door on the right led into the shop; it was bolted top and bottom.

Dawlish went quickly upstairs. He couldn't close the street door properly, but it was latched; no one glancing at it casually would know that the lock had been forced. He reached the landing, which was small and narrow and led to a passage. Three doors led off this, and at the far end was another flight of stairs.

The light came from an open door—from the room at the front of the shop. No other light was on, and there wasn't a sound in the house. Dawlish hesitated for a moment, then walked to the foot of the stairs and looked up; only darkness met him.

He heard a sound, in the house, above him. He raced up the stairs, and a door slammed. He opened it cautiously, and found a dark room. Clanging sounds came from an open window; when he reached it, he saw two men disappearing into the night. The window led to a fire-escape. There was nothing he could do.

He swung round and went into the front room.

A man lay on the floor, in a corner, with his head smashed in.

Dawlish stood quite still, and looked; nothing was good to see. The man had been savagely attacked. Blood had soaked into a pale-coloured carpet, and there were splashes on the wall near him. He had obviously been sitting at a roll-top desk, which was open and littered with papers. They seemed to have been tossed about everywhere; a few were on the floor, and blood glistened on several of them, like red-ink spots.

This man had not been dead long.

Dawlish went across to him, and felt his pulse; it was a waste of time, except that it told him he was right. The man hadn't been dead for long. His hand still had its natural warmth; the blood wasn't clotted, as it would have been had it been exposed to the air for an hour or more.

He turned to the desk. On top were several old books, and in bookshelves which lined the walls there were dozens more. The room was part study and office.

Dawlish bent down, and looked in the man's pockets; he found the wallet half out of its pocket, so the man's clothes had probably been searched. Then he saw a piece of paper, poking out of the left sleeve, as if it had been pushed up there, out of sight. Dawlish took it out, gingerly so as to avoid leaving prints; it was the start of a letter. It began:

"To the Assistant Commissioner of Scotland Yard.
"Sir,
    "I am writing this in case—"

That was all; but it said plenty.

Dawlish left it, for the police to find, put on a pair of cotton gloves, and rummaged about until he found a locked drawer with a lock forced. He pulled this open. There were several rubber bands inside, the kind of bands which might be slipped round a bundle of treasury notes. There was no safe and no cash-box in the desk.

Dawlish stepped over the dead man's body.

As he did so, he glanced towards the open door and the landing. He heard no sound, but saw a shadow; it would have been a complete surprise, had the light not been on. The shadow was on the floor near the door, vaguely the shape of a man's head.

There was still no sound.

Dawlish showed no sign that he had noticed anything, and turned back to the desk. There he couldn't be seen unless the man came right into the room. He picked up some papers as he passed the desk and reached the wall. He crept towards the door. The shadow was no longer in sight; and the uncanny silence lingered. It was possible that he had surprised the murderer, who was already half-way down the stairs. He had let this happen, and might now be letting the murderer get away.

He glanced at the window, rustling the papers as if he were still at the desk.

He would surely hear the front door open, would have time to reach the window and make sure that—

The top of a man's head appeared, round the door; a dark head. It was withdrawn immediately. Dawlish continued to rustle the papers, and coughed slightly. The head appeared again, the man could see into most of the room but would have to come farther before he could see the desk or Dawlish. Dawlish kept his right hand tight about the gun. He didn't want to shoot the man in the head; he wanted him alive.

The man's hand showed; and a gun in it.

Dawlish coughed again, rustled the papers—and then jumped forward. He kicked the door against the man outside, heard the gasp of pain, dodged as the door rebounded and slipped round it. The man was staggering back, hand at his face, the hand with the gun pointing towards the floor. Dawlish hit him; the blow caught the man on the chin and sent him rocking back on his heels. Dawlish struck again, and the man fell and went limp, the gun dropping from his grasp.

Dawlish looked down on a dark-haired man—just dark, not black-haired—wearing a light-brown suit.

He could telephone Trivett, and hand the man over. Trivett was the best officer at the Yard to get information out of this fellow. Or he could try to get that information himself and risk running into trouble with Trivett. He stood watching the little man, whose lips were bleeding—he'd bitten them involuntarily as Dawlish had hit him. He had a sallow face and long, dark lashes, and a scar on the side of his chin.

Dawlish decided to make a start himself.

He lifted the man bodily, carried him into the room and dumped him into a chair. Then he felt his pockets and clothes and made sure there was no other weapon. He went back for the gun, and slipped it into his left-hand pocket; now he wouldn't be able to claim that he wasn't protected. He still felt savage fury with himself, because he was sure that the murdered man would still have been alive if he had come straight here.

He assumed it was Charles Oliver. He had never been told what the man looked like, but who but the tenant would be sitting at that desk, in his shirt-sleeves?

He went into the other rooms on this floor; one was a dining-room, the other a bedroom; there was a double bed, made-up oddments on an old-fashioned dressing-table, and several dresses hanging on hangers in the wardrobe; a woman's hat was on the bed, and two pairs of shoes, one shoe on its side, on the floor at the other side of the bed. So presumably there was a Mrs. Oliver.

He returned to the office.

His captive was stirring; his eyelids were flickering. Dawlish went across, took everything out of his pockets, pulling him forward in the chair to get at the hip pockets.

He kept a set of keys, and noted the man's name and address, on a letter. His name was Corby, and he lived in Dean Street, Soho.

Dawlish pulled up a chair and sat down, the wrong way round, so that he could fold his arms and lean against the back of it. He held his gun in his left hand, casually. He lit a cigarette, awkwardly, and put the lighter away as the man's eyes opened.

He didn't know where he was, and was still dazed. Dawlish didn't speak, but watched him and saw the dawning of consciousness and of recollection. The man licked his sore lips; the trickle of blood had run right down his collar now, and inside his collar. He didn't open his eyes wide, but slowly closed them again; foxing.

Dawlish stood up, backed to the desk and, covering the man with the gun, took off the receiver and dialled one letter—the last but one on the dial. The burring sound as the dial went round sounded very clear and long. The ringing sound was stilled when he lifted the receiver to his ear, but the prisoner wouldn't know that.

"Get me the police—in a hurry," Dawlish said.

He saw the other's eyes open, the man licked his lips again, and said:

"You'll be sorry." The man could hardly speak, because of his bruised lips; but the expression in his eyes told Dawlish that he believed he was telling the truth. Dawlish put the receiver down slowly, and strolled back towards the man, stood in front of him, towering as a giant over a pigmy. Already one unexpected fact had registered; the man was dressed in clothes of American cut, but spoke with an English accent.

"Now what?" asked Dawlish.

"Deverall—did that," said the man in brown. He nodded towards the corpse.

He looked frightened; it was even possible that he was frightened enough to tell the truth. It was difficult to be sure. Dawlish didn't move, but said:

"That's a lie."

"Think so?" The man tried to sneer, as if he were less frightened now. "You'll change your mind. Deverall was here. His finger-prints are all over the place."

"That doesn't make him a killer. You're here."

"I didn't do it! Deverall did! He won't have a chance."

"You're not having a good time," said Dawlish. "You haven't a chance, Corby. You—"

"I came *after* you," Corby said. "And I can prove it." Fear had gone, with his gathering confidence, and he was quite sure of himself. "So you'll be in a jam, too, Dawlish."

"That's right. See this gun?" Dawlish took the other's gun out of his pocket. "The bullet taken from a Bentley's tyre and the bullet on the road outside the American Embassy came from that. Not so good, is it? You shouldn't run around shooting people."

"*He* wasn't shot," said Corby. "I didn't croak him, either. Deverall did that."

The accusation came out flatly, this time, as if there wasn't the slightest doubt about its truth. The man shifted his position, licked his lips again, and sneered.

"Why don't you give it up, Dawlish?" he said.

"Yes, why don't I?" He turned round, went to the telephone, and dialled a number: Whitehall 1212. He saw the fear leap into his prisoner's eyes. The man actually jumped out of his chair and came across the room. Dawlish moved the gun, and checked him.

"Superintendent Trivett, please."

Corby cried, "You fool!"

"That's right," said Dawlish. "Don't come any nearer. . . . Hallo, Bill? . . . Yes, your *bête noire* again. I should come to Stenway's place if I were you. There's been more trouble. . . . I don't think I can stop, but bring a squad; you'll need everything for homicide."

He replaced the receiver, and Corby stood in front of him, quivering; with rage or with fear? Dawlish wasn't sure which.

"You fool! Now Deverall—"

"We'll look after Zeb later on," said Dawlish. "Turn round."

Corby obeyed; his face was livid. Dawlish caught his right arm behind him in a hammer-lock, then turned him easily and marched him towards the door. Corby was still trembling, more now because he didn't know what to expect next. Dawlish took him to the stairs, and they started to go down. At the foot he told the man to open the door, and Corby obeyed, without argument. It struck cool outside, and a wind had sprung up in the last half-hour. Dawlish marched Corby along the poorly lit street towards the spot where his car was parked. No one who passed in the wider street seemed to notice anything unusual; the light wasn't good.

"Get in," said Dawlish, and opened the door.

Corby obeyed.

Dawlish slammed the door on him. He might try to run while Dawlish was going round to the driving-seat. He didn't, possibly because his arm hurt so much. Dawlish put his gun in the dashboard pocket, and drove away. He went towards Mayfair, and kept to the side streets; in less than fifteen minutes he was drawing up in a mews, not far from Oxford Street, where Tim Jeremy had a flat.

Dawlish had a key to the flat.

There was a flight of stone steps leading to the front door. Two lights burned over the doors of lock-up garages; the mews had only one other residential flat, and that was at the other side.

He didn't man-handle Corby again, but opened the door and stood aside.

"Hurry," he said.

Corby obeyed.

Dawlish found the light-switch, pressed it down, and stood outlined against the doorway as Corby went uncertainly into the rectangular hall. The living-room was on the left, a bedroom on the right; other bedrooms and the domestic quarters were straight ahead.

Dawlish closed the door behind him, as Corby turned round.

"I thought you'd want to do a deal," he said.

"Did you?" asked Dawlish mildly. He went forward, pushed open the door of the sitting-room, and stood aside for Corby to enter. Corby thought he wanted to do a deal; that explained his confidence and his willingness to come without making trouble. Corby was going to get a shock. "Now let's see," said Dawlish. "Where's Deverall? You can have five minutes, and if you haven't talked by then I shall beat you up. Cheerfully and painfully. Understand?"

TWELVE

CORBY

Dawlish went across to the largest arm-chair in the room and sat down. It had been bought for him at a time when he and Tim had shared this flat. It was a large room, furnished for comfort as well as with taste. By the side of Dawlish's chair was a cupboard with a radio on the top. He opened the cupboard and took out two bottles of beer and two glasses.

"One minute gone," he said. "Have a drink?"

Corby came forward slowly. Dawlish picked up a bottle, took the cap off, and poured out; he poured the beer into a large glass, and handed it to Corby, who drew back.

"Don't get any ideas about throwing that at me. Where's Deverall?"

He didn't know it, but his expression was rather like Rudolph Meyer's had been, that afternoon. His face was blank and his lips set, and the real effect was in his eyes; he looked merciless.

Corby drank half his beer, and looked at Dawlish nervously.

"We can *prove* Deverall killed Oliver," he said.

"Not to my satisfaction."

"There's blood on his clothes, his finger-prints are all over the flat. Don't make any mistake. Deverall will hang if I talk."

"And according to you, even if you don't talk," said Dawlish softly. "You didn't bring prints away with you. You persuaded Deverall to go with you to that shop, and you think you've framed him for Oliver's murder. You haven't. You've less than half a minute left, and if you don't start talking, you'll know what Oliver felt like when someone started to batter him over the head."

Dawlish looked at his watch and stood up. Corby's eyes darted to and fro; his lips were swollen, and the cut over one eye looked ugly and raw. He fingered it gingerly, and backed away.

"Don't!" he gasped. "Don't, I'll tell you, I'll tell you! Give me a chance, give me a chance."

Dawlish drew back, turned his back on the man, and sauntered across to the chair. He didn't turn round, deliberately; he was giving Corby his chance. Corby took it. He advanced suddenly, with nervous speed, grabbed an upright chair and swung it. He jumped forward to bring the chair down on Dawlish's head. Dawlish stepped to one side, and the chair smashed against the floor. Corby, off his balance, ran into another punch from Dawlish's right hand; it shook his teeth. He tried to get away, but Dawlish buffeted him on either side of the head. The blows weren't hard, but they came with merciless regularity, and the attack lasted fully a minute.

Dawlish drew back, and poured himself out a glass of beer.

"Where's Deverall?" he asked.

Corby, still swaying beneath the rain of blows, put out a hand to support himself against a chair, and lowered himself into it. He had no strength left and no courage. He began to speak.

He gave an address in Soho; not his own, but a flat above a small shop. He looked too frightened to lie, and was gasping for breath when he had finished. Dawlish didn't wait to question him about anything else, but tied him hand and foot, thrust a handkerchief into his mouth as a gag, and carried him, mute and terrified, into the kitchen. He shut him in the larder, locked the door, and then left the kitchen. He didn't go back to the living-room, but went out, slamming the door, and ran down the steps. The mews was well lighted, and no one was about, as far as he could see. There were several dark corners, and he peered at each one as he went to the car and took the wheel. He drove out, went a hundred yards towards Oxford Street, parked the car round a corner, and hurried back to the mews. It was still silent and deserted, and no one had gone up to the front door; no one would have had time to get in without a key.

He walked swiftly back to the car, looked in the back, made sure no one was crouching down there, and drove towards Oxford Street and then Soho.

Trivett would find Deverall's finger-prints at the Niven Row shop, so obviously Deverall had been framed for the murder of Charles Oliver. If Corby had told the truth, Zeb was with one other man in the Soho apartment, and the other man would hardly expect a visitor—except Corby.

Dawlish had Corby's keys.

He turned into Shaftesbury Avenue and drove to Greek Street, left the car near a corner, and walked to Mill Street, a short thoroughfare only fifty yards away. He wanted Number 17—a tailor's shop, according to Corby. Bales of cloth and a dummy figure draped with cloth were in a window, visible in the light which came from a street-lamp a little way off. The street was narrow and deserted; a few lights shone at the windows of the higher storeys, but none at street-level. There was no light on above the tailor's shop. Dawlish unlocked the street-door and stepped inside a dark passage. He closed the door, and stood listening; he had made no sound.

He heard none.

He waited, hoping that his eyes would soon become accustomed to the darkness, but they didn't; there was no light anywhere, no faint diffusion which would enable him to see. So he struck a match; the rasp of the head on the side of the box sounded like a saw on metal. He narrowed his eyes against the glare, then saw the stairs, leading straight up—it was very like the place at Niven Row, but smaller; and there was a smell of stale cooking and of smoke, not fresh tobacco smoke, but smoke which suggested that the place hadn't had an airing for a long time.

The match went out.

He didn't light another, but went to the stairs, groped his way up, and thought hard. Had Corby lied? He had believed that the man was too frightened to lie, but—why was no one here? Or had he been seen? Was there a reception party waiting?

He reached the landing, and although he moved his great bulk with uncanny silence, could not prevent a loose floorboard from creaking. He stood quite still, listening, but there was no responding sound, nothing to suggest that the apartment was occupied. He struck another match; there were three doorways and another flight of stairs. He went up these and up a third flight, still in darkness. On the top floor he started to go into the rooms, switching on the lights as he did so. They were workrooms; sewing-machines and all the other equipment of the tailor's craft were there. He came upon a big hand-press, a bench with tailor's irons; everywhere there were clothes in some stage of manufacture. Not until he came down to the floor above the shop itself did he find the living-rooms. The first was large, furnished with cheap modern furniture; it had obviously been occupied recently, as an evening paper lay open on the floor by the side of an arm-chair.

It was so quiet; an uneasy quiet.

He turned towards the door.

A woman *screamed*.

The scream came shrill and piercing, beating against his ears, setting his heart racing. He jumped towards the door and opened it—and the woman screamed again. He could see no one. The light was behind him, and cast his own gigantic shadow against the wall above the stairs.

The woman screamed a third time.

The scream came from a room on this floor; from a door which was ajar. No light showed from it. He hurried along towards it, but there was silence now, deep and profound; as if he had been imagining the sounds he had heard. The screams kept echoing in his mind, like a gramophone record with the needle stuck at the same spot. He pushed the door open and stepped into a dark room—and the scream came again, not far away; ear-splitting. He groped for the light switch. He heard nothing else, but his ears were too full of that scream to hear. He touched the switch and pressed it down—and no light came.

He took a step farther into the room; and stopped. He did not know what made him stop. He hesitated, with one foot in front of the other, the dark room in front. Then he knew why he stopped; because it was so dark. It shouldn't be dark like this, because there was a light behind him—anyone coming up the stairs would be able to see him—but darkness blanketed the room.

He drew back.

The scream didn't come again, there was only silence.

He took out his own gun, pointed it towards the ceiling, and fired. The flash lit up a yard of space between him and a dark cloth curtain—he didn't realize that it was a curtain, only that it was something dark immediately in front of him. Then he heard a gasp and a thud of footsteps. He struck a match, and saw that it was a curtain, hanging from the ceiling. He tugged at one side, but it was fastened to the wall there. He darted to the other side and pulled, then moved back. There was no shooting, but he heard a scraping sound and a grunt; then a thud, farther away. He wrenched at the curtain and it moved back easily on runners. Faint light now showed a large room, with half a dozen divans with their heads against the walls; all were empty. The room was full of tobacco smoke, but it was a sickly smell, not of ordinary tobacco.

The window was open.

He heard footsteps below, went across and peered out. There was a small yard, and a vague figure disappeared through a gate in a wall—probably into the yard next door. The footsteps faded, and yet the quiet of the night was broken by the sounds of traffic not far off, and of footsteps some distance away.

In the house there was only silence.

On the floor by one of the divans was a hat; a wide-brimmed hat, not quite a Stetson, but more familiar in the United States than here. He recognized it, and had no doubt that it was Uncle Zeb's. He had no doubt what this room was, either; a pipe-dream parlour. Addicts came here and smoked and rested on the divans and had their dreams. The thick curtain was to muffle sound. A man and a woman had been on the other side of the cloth, waiting for him to step into it, to be muffled up in its folds. He didn't guess what would have happened then. It had seemed uncanny but it was simply explained—and if the hat were a true guide, Deverall had been here. If Trivett had come and found it, he might have taken it for granted that Uncle Zeb had come to smoke and dream, dropping his hat on the floor before he settled down. Father and son, marihuana dopes— could Trivett be blamed if he thought that?

Dawlish picked up the hat.

He would soon have to chose between telling Trivett everything he knew and acting on his own. Even if he told Trivett, he wouldn't stop the hunt for Uncle Zeb. He had known Uncle Zeb for a few hours and liked him, but he didn't know him well enough to be sure of his character. No one could look less like a dopy than Zebadiah, and no one looked less like a fool. It was possible that Zebadiah had told his story of the reason for his trip to England simply to fool Dawlish. Possible but—pointless. Was it even worth thinking about?

Dawlish picked up the hat and went out of the room. The only place worth searching was the lounge, but he didn't waste much time there. He found some letters addressed to Corby and others addressed to a man named Bligh; love-letters. He didn't trouble to take them away, made as sure as he could that he had missed nothing, and went towards the stairs.

As he reached the landing a car pulled up outside, doors slammed, and three or four men came towards the front door.

He heard Trivett's voice.

THIRTEEN

URGENT REQUEST

Dawlish backed away from the stairs as light flashed out from a torch. He went into the dream-parlour and crossed to the window as men came up the stairs. He climbed out, and dropped to the ground; it wasn't far. He had to climb two walls before reaching the street.

The wind was cutting fiercely from the corner. Only one man stood by the police car, no one else was about. Dawlish walked briskly to his car, put the hat on the seat by his side, and wondered whether to go back and see Trivett, or to go to Tim Jeremy's flat. He decided he did not want another talk with Trivett face to face. As he drove towards the West End his face was twisted in a smile which wasn't of amusement. He could not have done more to make absolutely sure that Uncle Zeb was hunted by the police; even if they didn't immediately trace him to Niven Row, they would be on the watch, for the Home Secretary would have been in touch with the Assistant Commissioner by now. Irony! He couldn't see through the fog of events, except one thing; that someone meant to frame Uncle Zeb for murder, and was making a pretty good job of it.

Unless Uncle Zeb *had* committed that murder.

The suspicion was seeping into his own mind.

He let himself think of the speed with which the police had arrived at the tailor's shop. They must have found evidence that someone connected with the murder of Oliver had gone there; and if that were so, it looked as if the evidence had been planted to make sure that the police would find Uncle Zeb's hat. The police would have certainly read Oliver's unfinished letter now.

Uncle Zeb certainly wouldn't have left his own hat deliberately; this was a frame, but proving it would cause some headaches.

It wasn't too late to see Trivett and tell him everything; Trivett would suspect, even if he didn't know, that Dawlish had been to the tailor's shop. He was at the cross-roads; cross-roads he'd often paused at before. The choice lay between telling Trivett everything he could, or carrying on by himself. The only justification for carrying on solo came from the possibility that he would get results more quickly than Trivett.

He reached Tim's flat, and the headlights lit up the mews, threw the roofs of the old stables, now converted into garages, into sharp relief. The night was cloudy and dark, and the wind blustered through the arch and made eddies in the corners, flinging dust and a few odd pieces of paper about.

He let himself in with a key, but didn't step forward immediately. He waited, ears strained, and caught no murmur of sound. He slipped inside quickly and stepped to the side of the door.

The silence was as great as it had been at the tailor's.

He went along to the larder, unlocked the door and looked in. Corby's eyes glistened, but Dawlish was in no mood to talk to him. He locked the man in again and went to the living-room, thrust open the door and switched on the light. Nothing moved, no one was there. He made a round of every room, gun in hand;

it was empty all right. He smiled at his own fears, returned to the living-room—and started.

The telephone bell began to ring; and unless his nerves were strained to their limit it wouldn't have affected him.

He flung the hat on to a chair, went across to the telephone, and lifted the receiver. He spoke harshly, in a voice no one was likely to recognize.

"Hallo?"

"Is that—is that Mr. Timothy Jeremy's flat?"

The voice was familiar, but Dawlish couldn't place it.

"Yes."

"Is Mr. Jeremy in?"

"I'm sorry, no."

"I wonder," began the caller, and paused; and in the pause, recognition of the voice came to Dawlish like a flash of light. "I wonder if you happen to know where I can find Mr. Dawlish? Mr. Patrick Dawlish. I know that Mr. Jeremy is a friend of his, and that Mr. Dawlish is in London, so I wondered—"

"He'll be here in an hour's time," said Dawlish.

"Really. Oh, good. My name is Meyer, Rudolph Meyer. Will you tell him I'll be round in an hour? One hour exactly. Thank you so much. Good-bye."

Dawlish put the receiver down slowly. He caught sight of the hat, and pictured it askew on Uncle Zeb's head. He went across, picked it up, and took it into the bedroom, putting it on top of the wardrobe.

The telephone bell rang again.

He helped himself to some beer before answering it; the caller was persistent, and at last he lifted the receiver, sat back with the tankard in one hand and the receiver in the other, and used the harsh, unrecognizable voice.

"Hallo?"

"Who's that?" asked a woman quickly.

Dawlish relaxed, smiled broadly, put the beer down and spoke in his natural voice, close to the mouth-piece.

"Your daring lover! Light of my life, how did you know I was longing to hear your voice? Beloved, where—"

"Pat, don't fool," said Felicity, but her voice held laughter. "At least, tell me all that some other time. I've just had a mysterious message from a mysterious woman, so I'm not in a romantic mood. She's *desperately* anxious to see you. Her name is Meyer," said Felicity. "Mrs. Rosa Meyer. She telephoned to ask if she could see you and was prepared to drive down here tonight. I said I thought you were staying in London and would let her know if I could give her your address. She left her number. It's Mayfair 23123."

"Thank you, my sweet. How are things?"

"Homer's quite all right again, now, except that he says he feels rather as if he's in the middle of a mild hangover. Elvira—" Felicity paused, and lowered her voice; Dawlish could imagine her glancing at the door, and putting her lips very close to the mouthpiece. "Pat, I don't understand Elvira. She's very bright— brittle bright."

"On the whole, I think you've a bunch of strange relations," said Dawlish lightly. "I'm not sure that I trust them all."

"There can't be anything *wrong*," protested Felicity. "I mean, with them. They—"

"Once a Deverall, always strictly reputable! I know. Still, Uncle Zeb married, you know, and his wife may have had a disturbing effect. Wives do, sometimes. Upset mental balance, moral standards, all that kind of thing. Why," went on Dawlish, waxing warm, "I've known at least one wife who always does her husband good, and whose voice always cheers him up. But that's unusual. Good-bye, sweet."

"Pat—"

"Oh, I'm awfully sorry, I shan't be home tonight," said Dawlish. "Bless you."

He rang off, held his finger on the cradle of the telephone, and lifted it again a moment later; that moment had been filled with a vision of Felicity, and it was a good vision. Then he dialled Mayfair 23123, and listened to the dialling sound, gazing at the ceiling with his expression blank; he didn't even blink.

A woman answered. "Hallo?" She spoke almost breathlessly, as if she had rushed to the telephone and was expecting a call.

"*Good* evening, Mrs. Meyer," said Dawlish brightly. "My name is Dawlish, and I understand—"

"Mr. Dawlish!" she cried. "Thank God! Mr. Dawlish, I must see you, it's desperately urgent. Where are you? May I come and see you right away?"

"I'm at Number 1, Hay Mews, Mayfair. But—"

"It's only ten minutes from here. Please—"

"I'll look forward to meeting you," said Dawlish primly. "*Au revoir.*"

She would almost certainly be here within ten minutes. It was now a quarter past ten. Meyer himself would probably be punctual, and that would bring him here at about five minutes to eleven. It might be amusing to confront them with each other.

Trivett might come, too. He might first telephone, to find out who was in; more likely he would call in the hope of catching Dawlish by surprise. If the Meyers were here and Trivett arrived, it would be a pretty scene.

He dialled Whitehall 1212.

"Is Superintendent Trivett in, please?"

"No, sir, he's not here, but he will be telephoning to pick up messages in a few minutes' time."

"Oh, good," said Dawlish. "Tell him Dawlish called, will you, and is very anxious to see him tonight but can't get to the Yard until twelve. I'll gladly come then—or if he would prefer it, I'd see him at Mr. Jeremy's flat. I'll be there just before twelve."

"Mr. Jeremy's flat? Will the Superintendent know it?"

"Oh, yes."

"I'll give him the message, sir," said the operator.

Dawlish rang off, and as he sat back, heard a taxi draw up, just outside the mews. He waited for a moment, and heard a woman hurrying towards the flat. The light from this room would show her the steps quite clearly. He got up and went into the kitchen, opened the larder door, and saw Corby's eyes, glittering; the gag and the bonds were still in position. Dawlish checked them, without speaking, and when he drew back the front-door bell rang.

"I'll be seeing you," said Dawlish. "I'll make you more comfortable soon."

He shut and locked the door.

He hurried out of the kitchen, leaving the light on. Before he reached the door the bell rang again; Mrs. Meyer was certainly bubbling over with urgency. He switched on the hall light, to see her better, and opened the door slowly.

She stood with a hand on the bell push, lips parted, eyes bright and rounded.

She was a child—a beautiful child.

FOURTEEN

GIRL-WIFE

She stood quite still, except that her hand moved from the bell push and stretched out towards him. She wore a black dress, with a mantilla over her head, shadowing her face, softening its lovely lines. She looked no more than a child of sixteen or seventeen. She was small, almost tiny; and so beautiful that she looked unreal.

"You are—Mr. Dawlish?"

"Yes, Mrs. Meyer." He found it difficult to frame the 'Mrs.' "Please come in."

She slipped past him, and he closed the door.

"I'll lead the way," said Dawlish.

He went into the room and stood aside, watching her. Nineteen? Surely she couldn't be more. Her smallness made her seem younger, of course. She pushed the mantilla back from her head; she had long, dark hair, waving beautifully, glossy and black as a raven's wing. Her colouring was superb, her complexion flawless, and he had never seen such eyes— deep violet in colour, fringed with curling lashes.

She stretched out her hand again, and it was trembling.

"Come and sit down," said Dawlish, "and tell me how I can help you."

"Oh, you can help me," she said. There was no trace of an accent in her voice. At her breast was a spray of deep red roses; the perfect touch. All she needed, now, was a rose in her hair. She ignored his invitation, but touched his hand. "You can help me by helping my husband. He needs it desperately, and he says you've refused. I've come to—to plead with you, Mr. Dawlish. You *must* help him. He is in such danger."

"I didn't know that," said Dawlish.

She moved away, but didn't sit down.

"He wouldn't tell you; he's so brave. He wouldn't plead for himself. He says that a man of your calibre wouldn't listen to a *man* begging for help. He went to see you this morning, in great hopes, almost—almost cheerful. He came back—despairing."

It was hard to picture Rudolph Meyer despairing.

"What help does he need?"

"He told you, he—"

"He didn't tell me of anything that would affect him as you say he's affected."

"No—no, he wouldn't." She shook her head slowly. "He would come with a business proposition; he would be cool and collected, and wouldn't show his fear. But Mr. Dawlish, he's in deadly danger. Three times he has been attacked. Three times! Tonight—" She caught her breath. "Tonight, I thought they had killed him."

She turned away, and he was sure that tears glistened in her eyes. She was pathetic and touching, but—it was impossible to take her at her face value. She actually turned her back to him, stretched out a hand and groped for a chair, touched it, and sat down. She leaned back with her eyes closed.

There was no sound in the flat, none outside. Dawlish stood

and looked down at her, his pulses stirring. Warning shrieked at him: not to believe her, not to be fooled. Meyer wanted to distract him from Uncle Zeb and had failed with direct approach, so he had sent his wife as a messenger, believing that few men could refuse anything she asked.

She opened her eyes, and spoke. Her voice was husky.

"A man broke into our house, and shot him. He was wounded in the shoulder. I thought—he would die."

Could that be true?

"Did you go to the police?" Dawlish asked.

"No," she said without hesitating. "I begged him to, a week ago, when it began. He said this wasn't a matter for the police. Some of them are his friends, but he wouldn't go to them. I don't know why. I do know that he thought suddenly of asking you for help, and felt convinced that it would solve the terrible problem. Then you refused, and I—"

She broke off, and closed her eyes again.

"Where is he now?"

"In bed," said Mrs. Meyer. "I made him go to bed."

"Has he seen a doctor?"

"Oh, yes."

"Didn't the doctor insist on going to the police?"

"No—no, he is a friend of Rudolph's. Mr. Dawlish, please help him. You don't know him well. If you did you would realize that he deserves help. He's so kind, so helpful to others; he thinks so little of himself. It hurts me terribly to see how much he is suffering. Please help."

"If it's as bad as this, I might try," said Dawlish almost reluctantly. "I'll have to see him. He'll have to tell me everything about this, including his reason for not going to the police. In the morning—"

"Please come tonight!" She was getting up slowly, her eyes

glowing. "I know I'm asking so much, but—please come tonight. I shall always be grateful, I shall never forget it, if you'll help him. It isn't far to our house."

"I can't leave here tonight—not until well after twelve, anyhow."

"I—see." She was standing in front of him again. "He might have gone to sleep then. Perhaps—what time in the morning?"

"Early."

"As early as you can, please."

"Is he in much pain?"

"He says he isn't," said Mrs. Meyer, "but he would say that, to help me. I think he must be in pain. He sent me out of his room, insisted that I should go to bed. He never likes it when I'm up late. But I couldn't rest, and I telephoned your wife. Mr. Dawlish—"

"Yes?"

"Need you tell him that I came? Can you come, pretending that you've changed your mind about not helping him?"

"I think perhaps I could," said Dawlish.

He glanced at his watch; it was twenty minutes to eleven, and Meyer should soon be here, if he were coming. The wounding, if it had really happened, must have taken place before Meyer's telephone call. It was nonsense to believe any of the story, and yet the way she had asked him not to betray the part she had played seemed wholly convincing.

If he kept her here until Meyer arrived, he would at least have a chance of finding out about that.

"And—you're sure you can't come tonight?"

"I might be able to postpone one of my appointments." He rubbed the bridge of his nose. "I wonder if you'll wait in another room while I telephone."

"Of course."

He led her across the hall to the little dining-room. She sat in a small easy-chair. He left her and closed the door.

He went back into the living-room, sat down, poured himself another beer, and lit a cigarette. In ten minutes Meyer should be here. There was no need to telephone. He need only wait for the minutes to fly; but they wouldn't fly. She would find the time drag more than he did. He went to the door at seven minutes to eleven, and half-expected to find her at the door. She wasn't. He went into the dining-room, and she jumped up.

"Can you come tonight?"

Her very heart seemed to be in her words.

"I'm not sure yet, but I'll know soon."

"Oh," she said. "You're very good. I'd rather wait until I know, but we mustn't return together. I'm afraid Bligh will tell Rudolph that I've been out, but if we don't arrive together he won't know that I came to see you. I hate deceiving Rudolph, but he insisted that I shouldn't take any part in this. In fact, he wants me to go away into the country until it's all over, but I won't leave him to fight it out alone. If I were sure he would have good help I might go."

That was neatly said.

"Who is Bligh?" Dawlish asked casually.

"Rudolph's secretary."

"I see." Dawlish rubbed the bridge of his nose again. "Well, you needn't stay in here any longer. Come into the other room, won't you?"

She went with him, and sat down in a chair facing the door; he saw to that. Then he went out with a murmured excuse, and opened the front door. He moved very quietly now, so that she couldn't tell where he was. As he looked into the mews, and his car parked there with the sidelights on, he thought of the name of Meyer's secretary: Bligh.

There had been letters addressed to a man named Bligh at the tailor's, as well as letters addressed to Corby.

He left the front door open, and went down the steps as a car drew up at the entrance to the mews. Dawlish stood and watched, heard a mutter of voices, but they were too far away for either to be recognized. Then a man approached the steps.

Rudolph Meyer was here, with his left arm in a sling.

"But how good of you to be waiting for me," said Meyer. They met at the foot of the steps, and the window of the living-room was closed, so that the girl-wife couldn't hear his voice. "In fact, it's good of you to see me again. Unless I felt it were really urgent I wouldn't have come to worry you, I wouldn't, indeed."

"That's all right. Do you mind keeping your voice low as we go in?"

"Not at all, not at all." Meyer dropped his voice to a whisper. "Someone asleep, no doubt, I quite understand. Gladly."

"What's happened to your arm?" asked Dawlish.

"Oh, an accident. Yes. I'll tell you a little more about it in a few minutes," said Meyer.

His whisper made him sound tired, and in spite of the glowing form of his words something of his buoyancy had gone; it was spurious now, as if he were forcing it against his inclination.

In the hall light he looked tired and flabby, and his eyes were dull, as if with pain; and bloodshot, too.

Dawlish put a hand to the handle of the living-room door and was about to open it when he heard a gasp, turned sharply, and saw Meyer swaying, as if he were going to fall. Dawlish grabbed his right arm, to steady him. Meyer had little colour, and his eyes were dazed. He still swayed. Dawlish let him sit down on a hall chair, and Meyer leaned his head against the wall and closed his eyes. If that were a faked attack of weakness it was brilliantly done.

"Can I get you anything?"

"No." Meyer's voice was barely audible. "No, thank you. Just a moment's rest and I shall be all right. I—I am rather weak. I lost a lot of blood earlier in the evening. But I had to come and see you. Dawlish, I beg you—"

He broke off, wincing.

Dawlish stood looking down at him, thinking of the girl-wife in the other room; and feeling as if he were as mean as men came. Meyer *was* hurt; it would be a sharp shock when he saw his wife.

Dawlish found himself smiling, grimly; he was getting soft-hearted where it would simply get him into trouble. He went along to the kitchen, and brought back a glass of water; Meyer sipped, and after a few minutes he started to get up. Dawlish helped him.

"Thank you—thank you." Meyer forced a mockery of a smile. "I shall be all right now, perfectly all right."

"Good."

Dawlish opened the door of the room, went inside first, deliberately, and stood aside. Meyer's wife still sat opposite the door, looking up eagerly, until Meyer came in.

Meyer stopped, his sound arm raised.

His wife cried, "Rudolph!"

Could two people act like this unless they were really astounded at seeing each other?

FIFTEEN

TALL STORY?

Meyer looked ill in the better light of the big room, and his eyes proved to be very bloodshot; he was hardly the same man who had been at Haslemere that afternoon. His mouth drooped and his chin sagged when he saw the girl, while she got up slowly. She reminded Dawlish of nothing so much as a girl who had disobeyed her father's instructions and who knew that she would be punished.

"Rosa," said Meyer, in a sighing voice. "My dear *Rosa*. Why did you come here?" He went across to her, his right hand held out, and took her arm. "Why did you do such a thing as this? Rosa, *why?*"

She didn't speak, and her eyes glistened with tears.

"Sit down, my sweet, and rest," said Meyer softly. "Don't be upset, I shan't be cross. I shouldn't have asked that foolish question. You did it to help me, of course. You came because you thought you might persuade Mr. Dawlish to help me. I shouldn't have told you anything about it; I should have insisted on your leaving London."

Rosa didn't speak, but sat down slowly. Meyer sat on the arm of her chair. She looked up at him, while he stared across at Dawlish, with reproach in his eyes.

"You wanted to surprise us both, of course. Yes, I can understand it, but—it's a shock. I thought Rosa was at home in bed. I sent her away from me because I didn't want her to know that I was coming out tonight, and I knew it would worry her. You'll be all right, Rosa my dear; both of us will be." The reproach was still in his eyes. "Have you told Mr. Dawlish everything?"

"Yes," said Rosa chokily. "Everything I know."

"That *is* everything," said Meyer. "Mr. Dawlish, my wife shouldn't be here. She ought to be at home in bed. Would you mind going to the front door and calling my secretary? Just call 'Bligh' and he will come. He drove me over here, and he's at the wheel of the car. I—"

Meyer broke off abruptly, shot a glance at his wife, then looked away again and went on as if he hadn't stopped; but he spoke more quickly. "I would like to send my wife home, and Bligh can come back for me later. That is, if you are still prepared to listen to what I have to say."

"I'll tell Bligh," said Dawlish.

"Thank you, thank you very much indeed."

Dawlish went out of the room, but not to the front door. He stopped and peered through the crack between the door and the wall. Meyer's good arm was round the girl's shoulders, and she peered up at him, worshipping him. Worshipping was the only word. It rang as false as hell and looked as genuine as a boy-and-girl love story. He went to the door and opened it.

"Bligh!"

"Coming," a man called at once.

He came briskly into the lighted mews, tall, well-dressed, youthful. He hadn't been with Corby that afternoon, and certainly wasn't wearing a suit of American cut. He hurried up the steps.

"He hasn't collapsed, has he?"

"Not yet. His wife's here, and he wants you to take her home."

"Oh," said Bligh. That was all. He followed Dawlish into the hall, and went ahead of him into the living-room. "I hope you're feeling all right, Mr. Meyer. You really shouldn't have come, you know."

"I'm all right, my boy." He put his hand to his head. "If my head didn't ache so much."

"Aspirins?" asked Dawlish.

"Well—"

"I'll get them," said Dawlish.

It meant leaving them all together, and he went noisily into the bathroom, but didn't get the aspirins; he crept back to the door.

"You ought to leave," Bligh said. "You'll make yourself really ill."

"Yes, Rudolph," Rosa said. "You really should."

"Later, later," said Meyer. "Please be quiet."

All sounded as innocent as could be.

Dawlish went to the bedroom, and had to hunt for the aspirins. He found them behind a bottle of hair-cream, and went back. Then he went for some water. Meyer took three aspirins, and said:

"Take Rosa home, Bligh, and ask Mrs. Harris to make sure that she goes to bed at once."

"Yes, of course." Bligh made no further protest.

Meyer stood up, and helped his wife to her feet. She walked obediently to the door, and Dawlish noticed that she evaded Bligh's eye. At the door she turned and looked at Dawlish, and the full flood of appeal was in her eyes, she moved her hand impulsively, and said:

"Please do everything you can."

She turned and went out, without waiting for an answer. Dawlish watched her go. Meyer followed her and Bligh out of the room. Meyer came back, alone; but not until the engine of the car outside had started up. He closed the front door with a bang, but came back slowly. His eyes were glassy now, as if from pain, and before he reached the chair he swayed again. He sat down heavily, and jarred his left arm; he winced, and his face was grey.

Dawlish mixed a whisky-and-soda and took it to him.

"Thank you," said Meyer. "You're very kind. I can't understand it, Dawlish, I really can't. Rosa—yes, it is the kind of thing she would do—she is so desperately worried about me, but—why didn't Bligh tell me she had left the house? He must have known. Why didn't he tell me? Why didn't he *stop* her? She is in as much danger as I am. These devils would kill her as readily as they would kill me."

He spoke between pauses, as he sipped his whisky, and his voice was hoarse. Finished, he lit a cigarette; he had a little colour now.

"But I needn't worry about Bligh now. I can tackle him when I leave. What did my wife tell you?"

"Danger. Shooting. Desperation. Fear."

"Yes, all that," agreed Meyer slowly. "She is very young, but difficult to fool. For weeks I thought that she had no idea that I was worried, but that was an illusion. She sensed it almost from the beginning, and eventually persuaded me to tell her a little. Not much, not everything, but a little."

"Why didn't you tell me all this, this afternoon?"

Dawlish poured himself another beer, but didn't drink much of it. Meyer's glass still held some whisky, but he had put it on a table by his side.

He smiled wryly.

"Why? Because I thought that I was a good judge of men, and couldn't bring myself to believe that you would accept my story at its face value. Mind you, I told you the truth, but only part of it. I *must* get those books. But I have no client for them; I want them for myself. *I* sold them to Stenway. They were in my own small collection, but I am thinking seriously of leaving England. It's a distressing thing, and it will be a painful wrench, but for my wife's health I ought to live abroad. She can only live in England for a few months in the year, and ought not to come here at all. She hates our being separated, however, and I confess I hate it, too. So, I made up my mind to retire. There were limits to what I could take with me, and while I am proud of my small library, books aren't my first love. So I sold them—practically all of them, keeping only those with a sentimental value."

He paused to sip his drink.

Dawlish looked at him without speaking and asked himself if this could be true.

"I sold them to Stenway," Meyer went on. "Soon afterwards I was—threatened. I must get the books back, or—I should be betrayed."

He used the word without emphasis, as if it were one which would arouse no great comment.

"Betrayed?" Dawlish echoed. "You mean, you were black-mailed?"

"Yes."

"What about?"

Meyer's eyes didn't change. He didn't look away, but stared at Dawlish as if defying him to disbelieve what was to follow. He spoke firmly and deliberately.

"Until ten years ago, Mr. Dawlish, I was a fence. That is, a receiver of stolen goods. I made a fortune. I shall not try to gain your sympathy, and you may think that I am being absurdly emotional when I say that I sickened of myself and my way of life. I withdrew completely. I started a reputable business, and was fortunate. Mr. Dawlish, when I retired from my first business, I had amassed a fortune of one hundred and fifteen thousand pounds. To make some amends, I have paid considerably more than that sum to charity in the past five years. But a life of crime is not one that can be banished. The past is the past, and mine was black. If it should be proved against me, I should go to prison. Rightly so, yes. I don't argue—but can I be blamed for wanting to avoid that?"

Dawlish made no comment, and Meyer went on:

"I do wish to avoid it, and if I can honestly, I shall. I have been able to assist the police on occasions, although I have never betrayed a man from whom I bought stolen goods in the past. I worked in the north of England mostly, and in France; I was not known in the south. I had been careful, and my true identity was known only to a few people. It was not until after I had sold these books to Stenway that I was made to realize that someone knew who was prepared to use it against me. That is the simple truth. I could not go to the police—I need not stress the obvious to you. I had to try to fight by myself. I have been attacked three times, but not hurt before. You know what happened tonight—a man broke into my house and fired at point-blank range. Had he wished, he could have killed me. He didn't want me dead, but wanted me to understand that he must have those books. He believes that I still have them, and—I most certainly have *not*. But I know who has."

Dawlish sipped his beer.

"Who?"

"Zebadiah Deverall."

"When did you find out?"

"My New York representative informed me a few days ago. He also told me that Deverall was coming to England. I found out what plane, and planned to be at London airport to meet him. Unfortunately he had made plans to leave at once, and I was a few minutes too late. By questioning some of the staff at the airport I discovered that he had instructed the driver of the car which met him to drive to Haslemere. I followed, and tried to think whom he should be going to see in Haslemere. It wasn't very difficult to follow, because they told me at the airfield that Deverall was in a Daimler hire car, a new one. In Haslemere I was told that a Daimler had gone towards Alum village. A little careful questioning, and the name of Dawlish was mentioned. I knew that I need look no farther."

Meyer sat back in his chair, strangely quiet and with unexpected dignity.

Dawlish examined the story, and found nothing that was improbable; everything could have happened exactly as Meyer had said. If it had, there was still a possibility that Meyer, Corby, and the other man dressed in American clothes were connected.

There wasn't any clear indication of that; the coupé had followed close upon the heels of the Daimler. The driver had not had to make inquiries at the airport, but had followed all the way.

Meyer raised his right hand and spread the fingers out on the arm of his chair. He sat forward a little, because of the risk of leaning against his injured shoulder. While telling the story he had recovered a little, but still looked a sick man.

"I hope you believe me," said Meyer. "I hope you understand why I invented a principal for whom I was acting. I hoped to avoid telling you or anyone the story of my first business. I was puzzled about your reaction, genuinely puzzled. Obviously

Deverall would not have come to see you unless you were already engaged in helping him. I should have imagined that you would have thought you could have obtained more information about the books by accepting my commission. Why *did* you refuse?"

Dawlish said owlishly, "I never like running with the hare and hunting with the hounds."

"I see, I see. You thought that I was the villain of the piece. I see. Well, I'm not, Dawlish. I am in your hands, too. I have given you information about myself which could do me great damage. You must use that information as you think best. Will you tell me one thing more: how did Deverall get in touch with you? Had he heard about you in the United States?"

"My wife's maiden name is Deverall."

"Really," said Meyer. "*Really!* How strange life can be! Am I right in assuming that he, too, had been menaced about these books? That the man who is blackmailing me is also trying to get them from Deverall? Two strings, so to speak, to his bow?"

"It looks like that. Meyer, who's blackmailing you?"

"I only wish I knew! I have no idea, I've tried to think. Desperately. Believe me, I don't know."

"Do you trust your servants?"

"Implicitly. In any case, none of them has any knowledge of my earlier life. Bligh, who has been with me longer than anyone else, just over five years, is a remarkably able man. I shall leave the remnants of my business in his hands when I take my wife out of the country. I trust him as freely as I would her."

"But you still wish you knew why he didn't tell you that your wife had left."

"Yes. I suppose there is a simple answer, but I do wonder, I do indeed. I will speak to him about it. Well, Dawlish!" Meyer tried to be brisk. "You now know everything. Presumably you are helping Deverall. *Will* you help me?"

SIXTEEN

GREGG

Dawlish moved away and wandered about the room. He paused by the radio and said in a casual voice:

"I'm already involved with the police."

"I understand that."

"It may not be possible to keep the story back—about your past, I mean."

"It is a risk I must take."

"It's a hell of a risk," said Dawlish. "You say your wife's a sick girl. Why not get out of the country at once? Go with her. Leave everything just as it is. You're not a poor man. You might lose a packet, but you'd gain peace of mind."

"I don't think so, Mr. Dawlish. I think they would follow me. They are so desperately anxious to get those books. Desperately." Meyer was fond of that word, yet uttered it without emphasis every time. The play-acting seemed to be over now, his behaviour as normal as it would ever be. "And I am afraid for—Rosa. You've seen her. You can understand that. They have concentrated their efforts on me, but they haven't forgotten her. No, indeed." He winced, as if in sudden pain. "They are working on her. They have named her, told me she will suffer, if I don't do what they want. As it is, she is greatly to be pitied. She has that dread scourge tuberculosis. She spends much time in Switzerland, sometimes in a sanatorium. She was released for this summer; they had hopes of a complete cure, but no—it's still there. Simister tells me that she isn't likely to live long—" He closed his eyes, and his voice was muffled. "Dawlish, don't make me talk like this. Don't!" He was trying to be fierce. "I told myself before I came to see you that maudlin sentiment would make no appeal to you. I can't help it. That child means more than life to me. More than life. But if. I were to die first, what would happen to her? I—"

The front-door bell rang.

Dawlish glanced round, and Meyer sat upright in his chair.

Dawlish expected Trivett; it was nearly midnight. He knew that Meyer's car would almost certainly be back by now; if the caller were Trivett, he might already know who was here.

"That may be a Yard man," he said abruptly.

"Oh," said Meyer. "You are working with them. I see. Well—I must leave it to you. Who is it likely to be?"

"Trivett."

"I know Trivett," said Meyer. "I should hate him to discover what I did in the past, but—I am in your hands." He stood up with an effort. "I have no objection to meeting him. There is just one request I must make, and I feel justified in hoping you will grant it."

"Yes?"

"*If* you decide that you must tell Trivett or anyone at the Yard, please inform me before doing so. Or at least immediately after you have done so. May I rely on you?"

"Yes," said Dawlish abruptly. "It won't be tonight. I'll make sure that this is Trivett."

He went out, leaving Meyer standing by the chair. He stood to one side as he opened the door; after tonight he was prepared for anything. It wasn't Trivett; it was Bligh, with another man, a small, rotund man, in a dinner-jacket and a black Homburg. Long before he opened his mouth Dawlish judged him as a fussy little man.

"Sorry to worry you, Mr. Dawlish," said Bligh. "I felt that I had to tell Dr. Simister that Mr. Meyer was here. He had instructed me to see that Mr. Meyer stayed in bed; he ought not to be out at all."

"I should think not," said Simister. He talked in a high tenor voice. "Absurd to think of coming out."

"He had a lot on his mind," said Dawlish, and led the way in.

Simister talked all the time, talked when he saw Meyer, reproved him, wagged an admonitory finger, took him gently by the sound arm and led him towards the door, as if he were prepared to get him out of the flat even in the face of physical opposition from Dawlish. It was foolish of Rudolph; he was old enough to know better. He had received a severe shock, and there might be complications. He was worrying his servants, and above all he was worrying his wife.

Meyer looked worse, after three minutes of that, than he had when he had first arrived. He said good night in a low, tired voice.

Bligh smiled as Dawlish saw them off.

Dawlish returned to the chair that had been made for him, lit another cigarette, stared at the glowing tip, and deliberately stubbed it out. He was smoking too many cigarettes, a sign of nervous tension. Yet he shouldn't be surprised that he felt keyed up. He closed his eyes and sat back.

A man approached the front door.

Dawlish stood up. The footsteps didn't sound like Trivett's, but it was nearly half-past twelve, and Trivett was probably here. He opened the door before the caller rang.

"Good evening, sir," said Detective-Sergeant Gregg. "Can you spare me a few minutes?"

"Cheerfully. Come in." Dawlish led the way into the living-room. "Sit down. How about a beer?" He looked amiable and lazy—and as fresh as if it were first thing in the morning, and he'd had a walk round the orchard. Gregg had the same fresh-ness; he was a likeable young man, rather like Bligh, in some ways; not facially, but in manner and openness.

"Well, that's nice of you. Thanks."

Dawlish poured out and offered cigarettes. He sat in the large chair, which Gregg had carefully avoided, and looked rather vacantly inquiring.

"My friend Trivett couldn't make it, then?"

"No, sir. It's been a heavy day, and there were some odds and ends he had to look after himself. I'm a poor deputy, I'm afraid." He drank his beer. "You got on to Oliver's murder pretty quickly, didn't you? He hadn't been dead much more than an hour when we reached him. We're very grateful for that tip. He might not have been found for a couple of days."

"Wife?"

"She's in the country with his mother. Had to leave in a hurry." Gregg frowned. "Nasty business, I'm afraid. She's expecting."

"Oh," said Dawlish heavily. He felt as if he had been kicked; and it hurt. He had been near when Oliver had died; had he gone into the flat sooner he might have saved that life. Now, somewhere in the country, a pregnant woman would soon have to be told that her husband was dead.

"Gets you rather, doesn't it?" murmured Gregg. "We were

there just after you left, of course. See anyone about?" He smiled, as if he couldn't imagine that such a thing was possible, but had to ask for formality's sake.

Corby was still in the larder.

"I didn't stay long there," Dawlish said.

"You couldn't have. Go to Mill Street?"

Dawlish smiled, his lips curving deeply at the corners. Gregg was no fool, and his very ingenuousness would make pitfalls for the wary.

"Yes," he said.

"Mr. Trivett said he was pretty sure you'd been there. Find anything?"

"I found a pipe-dream parlour."

"Empty, I suppose."

"Empty."

"Mr. Trivett said it almost certainly had been. Oh, he has authorized me to tell you the whole story as far as we know it." That was almost convincing. "We found several addresses at Stenway's place, and didn't lose any time getting across to Soho, which was among the places named. Deverall had been at both places."

"Sure?"

"Well, his prints were everywhere, and he certainly hadn't been there before tonight, had he? I mean, he arrived in England at about ten o'clock this morning, went straight down to your place, and didn't reach London until he came with you and then did that disappearing trick. So he went there, all right."

Taking the hat away hadn't been so clever, after all; if he'd had any sense, he would have wiped the doors to remove prints. There hadn't been time to do the job thoroughly, but he could have stayed long enough for that. The scream had unnerved him. Who *had* screamed?

"Any idea where he is now?" asked Gregg.

"I wish I had!"

"'Fraid you wouldn't have." Gregg was apologetic. "Still, we have to ask, you know. One way and another, you've had quite a day, haven't you? Must be feeling pretty tired. By the way, what did Meyer want?"

That was beautifully timed; at the moment when Dawlish was reflecting on the naïveté of a raw detective it came as smoothly as a whistle, and Gregg's eyes would miss nothing, for all the fact that the rather boyish smile was still on his lips.

"So you're watching Meyer," said Dawlish.

"Well, we pick up a few things, and you gave us a pretty clear warning about him, didn't you? Don't know the chap myself, although I've seen him once or twice. He knows more about rare books than anyone in England, I'm told, and this started off as a book problem. I wonder *why* this mysterious cove who's worrying Mr. Deverall is so anxious to get them. Any idea?"

"None."

"Pity." Gregg waved his right hand. "Hurt, wasn't he?"

"Meyer? Yes."

"What was the trouble?"

"I think you'd better ask him," said Dawlish mildly.

"Well, we don't want to tackle him yet," said Gregg apologetically. "The more information we can get about him the better, but we don't want to let him think we're suspicious. Accident, was it?"

"You can call it that."

"Oh, well," said Gregg, and chuckled. "Mr. Trivett told me I wasn't to force any questions. And I must be off!" He got up briskly, finished the beer left in his tankard, and moved towards the door.

A minute later Dawlish heard him walking across the mews.

Dawlish stood smiling thoughtfully, and admiring Trivett's tactics. Trivett knew Gregg's capabilities and hoped others would take him too much at his face value. Trivett was also suggesting that he had something far more important to do than interview Dawlish; it was a form of nerve war, which Trivett could play well. Trivett had let Dawlish know that he was aware of a great deal, and wanted Dawlish to think he had learned much of that because of Gregg's inexperience. Doubtless Trivett wanted him to assume that the Yard knew a great deal more than they actually did.

Trivett did not know about Corby. It was time he went to see Corby. He glanced at his watch; it was after one. He yawned again, and hoped that there would be no more disturbances for a while. He wouldn't finish with Corby until two, at least, and he had to make up his mind how to handle the man. One obvious way presented itself: to work on the Bligh angle.

He lit another cigarette and went along to the kitchen, but didn't open the larder door at once. He contemplated the plates, cups, and saucers on the dresser, and found two questions at the top of his mind. What had made Deverall walk out? And had Meyer told the truth? If he could answer those, he could probably answer everything else. He went across to the larder, deciding that he would soft-pedal with Corby. The man would already be in a pretty bad state both physically and mentally. Kid-glove tactics were indicated, and on the whole he preferred them to any other.

He opened the door.

He took a step back, and raised his hands; and alarm sheered through him.

He would not be able to use kid gloves on Corby; no tactics would help with Corby, whose throat was cut.

SEVENTEEN

FIXED

Dawlish shut the larder door and moved back, but even when Corby was out of sight the man's face seemed to leer at him. He leaned against the draining-board, and ran his hand across his forehead; it came away damp. Violent and sudden death wasn't new to him, but this hit him like a blow from a sledgehammer.

Three people had been in the flat, and out of his sight for a few minutes—long enough to have come along here and killed Corby, if they'd moved fast. It would be someone who had known or guessed where Corby was, and had moved fast. If only he had put the larder-door key in his pocket!

More vain regrets. Corby hadn't been able to make a sound in protest or do a thing to save himself. Someone had opened that door, and the helpless man had looked up and seen a knife and known what was coming.

The cold-blooded devilry of it began to make Dawlish seethe.

Meyer had been alone in the living-room, but only for a minute or two. His wife had been in the dining-room for over ten minutes. Bligh could have slipped out of the living-room while Dawlish had been hunting for the aspirins in the bathroom. Whoever it was had been pretty quick in finding Corby in the larder, but—they'd found him.

That was another possibility: that someone had forced a way in while Dawlish had been talking with the others.

He stood up—and the telephone bell rang.

He went along to the sitting-room, and by the time he reached it the ringing had stopped. That didn't worry him. He wasn't anxious to talk to anyone. Two men were dead, because of the way he had worked. Corby hadn't been worth much to anyone, but murder like that—

Oliver had been a decent, honest man, as far as he knew.

If he telephoned Trivett or Gregg, and told them, he would have to tell them everything. In any case, they would probably know who had been at the flat. All three suspects would be interviewed; Trivett couldn't let the night pass without seeing them. So the murderer would be warned immediately that the police were on the move against him—or her.

Could *Rosa* have used that knife?

It was almost a waste of time suspecting her; but it would be easy to be completely fooled by Rosa Meyer. He wanted to know more about Bligh and the fussy Dr. Simister. The quickest way to get it would be through Trivett; one of the newspapers would be the next best thing.

The telephone bell started to ring again.

"Oh, shut up," he growled, but lifted the receiver. "Dawlish speaking."

"That's fine," a man said. He spoke in a muffled voice, and there was nothing familiar about it. "Looked in the larder yet, Dawlish?"

Dawlish didn't speak.

"Silence gives consent," said the speaker in the same muffled voice. "I've fixed you, Dawlish, the same way as I've fixed

Deverall. Just keep your big hands off this job, I don't want any more interference. Keep away from Meyer—don't take any notice of his sob-story, or his sickly little wife's. Just forget it. Or—"

He paused.

"Tired?" asked Dawlish, and sounded almost flippant.

"No, I'm not tired," said the man with the muffled voice. "That job was done with a knife that belongs to you, Dawlish. Take a tip from me. Dump the body some place and forget the case. Go back to Haslemere, tell Homer and Elvira they've outstayed their welcome—that's *very* important—and look after your pigs. Don't forget."

The man rang off.

Dawlish rubbed the bridge of his nose, and his expression became more wooden than ever. He didn't know whether the man on the telephone seriously thought that he could be frightened off; it might be a good idea to let him have reason for thinking so.

If Trivett were told immediately, the inquiries would start, and the Meyer ménage would be under considerable pressure—and the more Dawlish thought about that, the more certain he felt that it wouldn't be a good thing. If he kept the body here until morning, and then started to work himself, he might get results. If he took Corby's body away, and dumped it, then the man with the muffled voice would think that he was scared.

His eyes were heavy, and he was thinking the same things over and over again. The wise thing was to sleep on it. He glanced at the kitchen door, where the light was still on, and grimaced. He put out the light there. Immediate action now wouldn't help Corby, and might harm Deverall.

He went into Tim's bedroom. He had a set of pyjamas at the

flat and everything he needed for the morning. He went to bed, and to sleep, thinking of the dead man in the kitchen and the fact that it was almost certain that one of three people had killed him. *Almost* certain.

He slept heavily.

He woke to a sunny morning and a cheerful sound from the mews; a man, whistling. He didn't get up at once, but lay looking at the window, and as he recalled what had happened the previous day he smiled wryly. Well, the whistler was bright and cheerful. What would he say if he knew that a murdered man was only a few yards away?

Dawlish got up, put on a kettle, and had to open the larder door to get the tea.

He had thought that he was more used to death by violence than most people, but this had done something to him, and his own share of the responsibility was largely to blame. He made tea, then bathed and shaved and began to dress. He had expected the telephone to start ringing by now, for it was after nine o'clock, but apparently no one was interested in him.

Tim Jeremy had three morning newspapers delivered, and they were poking through the letter-box. Oliver's murder was reported; two of the papers had spread themselves on it. There was a paragraph about a mysterious shooting incident outside the American Embassy; that was all that affected Dawlish. He didn't fancy going to the larder to get anything for breakfast, he hadn't yet made up his mind what to do. Tell Trivett? It seemed the only sensible thing, but the sensible thing so often lacked the little something that a case like this needed.

There was a café near by where he could get a snack, and—

He heard a faint sound at the front door. He was coming out of the bedroom, and until then had heard nothing—not even the joyful whistling, for the man had stopped. He drew back into the bedroom and peered round the door—and the sound was repeated; like a key scraping against the lock. A key?

He heard the lock click, and then saw the handle slide back slowly. He stood so that he could see but wasn't likely to be seen immediately the new-comer looked in—and his right hand was tight about his gun.

The door opened.

Elvira put her head round the door.

She glanced about the hall, and then disappeared. Dawlish heard her whispering; the sound came softly. Then she appeared again, opening the door wide, but behind her came Homer, who looked exactly as he had yesterday. Behind Homer came Timothy Jeremy, a tall, lean man.

Homer kicked against the door-mat.

"*Quiet!*" breathed Elvira. "Perhaps he isn't up yet."

Another whisper in a different voice came immediately.

"Don't wake him, he probably didn't get to sleep until the early hours."

That was Felicity; she was coming up the steps. So everyone from Four Ways was in London. Elvira, still leading, came softly into the hall. Homer was grinning slightly. Tim's face was expressionless, except for a droll smile which curved his lips but didn't touch his fine brown eyes.

By now Dawlish had withdrawn his head, and Elvira was getting nearer.

"Don't go in there," Felicity called in an urgent whisper. "Elvira, don't—"

Dawlish moved forward.

"Pat!" gasped Elvira.

"Who's springing a surprise on whom?" asked Dawlish brightly. "Good morning, all! You must have got up early."

He patted Elvira's arm, passed her, kissed Felicity lightly on the cheek, and gripped Tim's shoulder.

"How are you, darling?" asked Felicity.

"Blooming."

"You haven't had breakfast, have you?"

"No. But—"

"Sigh of relief," said Tim. "There should be something left for the rest of us, if it's only a snack. Elvira, you were boasting about cooking eggs and bacon. I have eggs and bacon, in the larder— far end of the kitchen, which is the door on the right. That is—" Tim broke off and looked at Dawlish in mock horror. "Unless you had a little snack here last night. If you had a little snack, it means we haven't a crumb left."

"I threw a party," said Dawlish promptly, and moved between Elvira and the kitchen. "Breakfast's off—or we have to have it out."

"But we can't," protested Elvira. "That's one of the things I can't understand about London; you can't get breakfast any where. In New York, now—"

"If you want to make an Englishman mad, say New York's better than London." Homer broke his silence, and was looking up at Dawlish with a crooked smile. "Isn't that so, Pat?"

"My dear chap, of course not. No Englishman ever believes any city in the world is better than London. It might be prettier, taller, faster, but not *better.*"

He was now in the kitchen doorway.

"We'll rustle up something to eat here," said Tim.

"Of course," said Felicity. "Mind, Pat, I'm hungry. We were up just after six. I wouldn't telephone you, in case you were asleep. Elvira and Homer felt that they had to come to London, they wanted to see—"

"Where *is* Dad?" asked Elvira suddenly.

"Sure, where's Dad?" asked Homer.

"Out," said Dawlish. "Fel, we'll breakfast out, too. I've been through the larder, there isn't enough to feed one of us."

"That," said Tim in a deep voice, "is slander."

"Nonsense," said Felicity, and pushed past Dawlish, towards the larder.

EIGHTEEN

BREAKFAST

It was only a step, and she would have the door open in a couple of seconds. Dawlish could grab her and prevent her from reaching it, and that would tell them all that there was some special reason for not wanting her to look inside. So he moved towards the dresser, and spoke as she touched the larder door.

"I won't stall. Uncle Zeb's missing," he said.

Felicity dropped her hand, and turned round. Elvira said, "What?" in a strangely hoarse voice. Homer behaved more naturally, and approached Dawlish, chin thrust forward aggressively.

"What do you mean?"

"What I say, I'm afraid."

"But—but he came with you," protested Elvira.

"He didn't stay. He walked out, at Scotland Yard, and I haven't seen him since."

"Have you looked for him?" Homer demanded.

"I've done what I can. The police are looking out. He wasn't forced to go, but went willingly."

"Why weren't we told?" Homer was abrupt.

"There wasn't anything you could do," said Dawlish.

"I just can't believe it," Elvira said in a husky voice. "Why should Dad do a thing like that?"

"That's one of the things I want to know," said Dawlish. "Only one. Remember Stenway?"

Homer's eyes narrowed.

"Sure."

"He had an assistant, who took over the shop and managed it for Stenway's wife. Oliver went the same way as Stenway last night. Just after your father had visited him, Homer. Sorry."

Homer's lips tightened for a moment, then he spat the words out:

"You saying Dad killed him?"

"I am not. I'm saying that your father went to visit him, without telling me where he was going, and soon afterwards Oliver was killed. Homer, I haven't been told everything about those books. At most it was half a story. Where are the books?"

"Still up in the attic," Felicity said.

"Sure, that's right." Homer's gaze was unfriendly. "I still don't like the way you said that, Pat."

"I don't like a lot of things. What's the truth?"

"You've had the truth. We came to you because we'd heard you were good," sneered Homer. "I don't think you're so good. Elvira, we're getting out of here."

"No, don't go." Felicity moved forward. "Pat's worried, obviously, and—"

"We like you," Homer said, "but we don't have to stay and be insulted by your husband."

He took Elvira's arm and hustled her out of the kitchen. She didn't speak and didn't look round.

"Pat—" began Felicity.

"Go with them," whispered Dawlish. "Sorry, my sweet, it was the only way, we've got to shake the truth out of them. Hurry!"

The front door was already open. Felicity didn't argue, but went along the passage. Homer shut the door, not knowing she was behind him. As she opened it again, Dawlish saw a lithe young man disappear from the entrance of the mews; it was Detective-Sergeant Gregg.

The door closed, and Dawlish went back into the kitchen. Tim ran a hand through his lank dark hair, smiled faintly, and lit a cigarette. Dawlish stood like a block of wood against the draining-board.

"Dawlish, the masterful," murmured Tim. "Why all this? Elvira's a nice girl, and I think the evidence is that Homer was framed in the car crash. Not convinced?"

"No," said Dawlish. "He could have been framed, but I wouldn't like to take it for granted yet. He is supposed to be F.B.I. I'd like to be sure. Things aren't too good, Tim."

"Deverall really on the run?"

"I think he's gone at the point of a gun, but can't be sure of that, either. I think he's being framed—that's also uncertain. The only thing I'm sure about is that he and his children haven't told us everything, and Felicity might be able to worm it out of them."

"Don't get me wrong, but I've never known you act like that without a better reason than that. What was it?"

Dawlish said: "I didn't want Felicity to see the body in the larder."

Tim's eyes narrowed; it was his only sign of surprise. He waited for a moment, then turned and went to the larder, opened the door and looked in. His hand slid down the side of the larder-door, slowly, then came away. When he turned round his expression was sombre.

"I see what you mean."

"I wish I saw what it meant. I wish I'd taken a look at the

books which they brought from America, too. Not that I'd be much help. I don't know anything about books." He stood frowning and looking into Tim's eyes. "I was going to ask you to get Old Silas to drop in and have a look at them this morning. Remember Old Silas? He runs a second-hand bookshop in Haslemere, and he'd tell us if the books are really valuable. I doubt if the police will let him in without one of us there. The police are still on duty, I take it?"

"Two—one back, one front."

"I'll telephone Allen," said Dawlish. "Close that door."

"You go and telephone," said Tim.

Dawlish went into the living-room and dialled TOL. He gave the number of the Haslemere Police, and was asked to hold on. Except for a few seconds, when he had first seen Felicity, he was as gloomy now as he knew how to be. At least he'd prevented Felicity from getting a shock; the body had to be removed before she came back, or before she went into the kitchen again.

"You're through," said the operator.

"Thanks. . . . Inspector Allen, please."

Dawlish held on, and heard sounds in the kitchen which at first puzzled him; they didn't puzzle him for long, for the smell wafted through. When there was a sizzling noise and a smell of frying bacon, it didn't take a genius to know what was happening. Trust Tim! Dawlish felt more cheerful already.

"Inspector Allen here."

"Aye, aye, sir," said Dawlish brightly. "Dawlish. Remember me? Trivett's being obliging and keeping me in London, but there's a little job you can do for me."

"Good morning," said Allen formally. "I'll help if I can."

"Thanks. In the attic at Four Ways there's a crate of books—a wooden crate, and you can't miss it. I wonder if you'd get Old

Silas to go along, have a look at them, and tell me if they're valuable. Just let me have a brief report—through you, of course."

"I see. I'll do that gladly."

"Thanks," said Dawlish. "All quiet down there?"

"Your wife and the others left early."

"Lucky man," said Dawlish.

He rang off. The smell was even more appetizing, and he reflected for a moment on the callousness of a hungry man. Then he went to see if he could do anything to help.

It was ten o'clock.

"Feel better?" asked Tim, leaning on the breakfast-table, and lighting a cigarette.

"Much. Almost human."

"Don't ask me to believe in miracles." Tim gave a lazy smile. "Well, I've been possessing my soul in patience, but I'd like to know what's been happening. That's if you don't mind. Also, what you propose to do with the body. Whose is it, by the way?"

"Chap named Corby." Dawlish lit his cigarette and then poured out another cup of tea. "He was at Four Ways yesterday, shot at me last night, and I think he probably murdered Oliver. As for what's happened . . ."

The story took twenty minutes, and he left nothing out except the frills. Tim nodded occasionally, grunted once or twice, but never interrupted the flow of the story.

"So what?" he said when Dawlish ended.

"Someone is being very clever. Rudolph Meyer, his wife, Bligh—odd about that name, I wouldn't have given much thought to Meyer's faithful secretary if it hadn't been for coming across the name Bligh before—or Uncle Zeb. I fancy that both Homer and Elvira know that Uncle Zeb hasn't been on the up-and-up. I think we can take it for granted that the trouble started with a set of old books, that Uncle Zeb has them, and somebody wants them. Also, Meyer once had them. If Meyer had them he wouldn't have let them go if he'd had any idea of their exceptional value, and that seems to support his story that a third party is after them. Puzzle—find the third party."

"Just as simple as that," murmured Tim.

"The complications only cloud the issue, including the fact that Oliver was writing to Scotland Yard when he was bumped off." Dawlish stood up abruptly. "Any ideas?"

"Yes. Tell Trivett. Everything."

"Funny how great minds *will* think alike," said Dawlish. He went across to the telephone.

Trivett was in his office.

At Dawlish's request they met at a little restaurant in Chelsea. Dawlish arrived last, and went upstairs to a small private room, which he knew of old. No one but Trivett was up there. No one unknown had followed Dawlish; had he been followed, Tim, who had come after him, would have warned him not to go in.

A waitress brought coffee.

"Now, what's all this secrecy about?" asked Trivett. "Or have you lured me here to bump me off?"

"Yes. Found Deverall?"

"No."

"Suspect him of Oliver's murder?"

"We can't rule him out. Is this a cross-examination?"

"Just an exchange of confidences between friends," said Dawlish brightly. "Any reason to suspect that Uncle Zeb is a bad man?"

"Except what's happened in England, no." Trivett sipped his coffee. "You did a good job at the American Embassy. We were looking for him before we discovered that we needed him for questioning. Not that it's done much good, Pat, but at least we've got off to a good start. I have no idea where he is or where he might be. We've discovered that the tailor's place was a dream-parlour, and found a lot of hashish under the floorboards. No one will smoke hashish or marihuana in that place again. We've also discovered one other thing, although I'm not sure I should tell you about it."

"No, Bill," said Dawlish humbly. "But I'm grateful for crumbs."

"It's all you'll get. Stenway and Oliver were together in a drug-racket. Among the books they shipped abroad or received from abroad and sent throughout the country there were always dummies. It was very cleverly done. Real binding was used, but the insides of the books were hollow, and packed with dope. Not only the pipe-dream stuff—cocaine and morphia as well."

Dawlish sat and looked at the Yard man. Trivett wouldn't lie; all this was simple truth—but almost too simple.

Homer had been on a drug investigation for his paper, perhaps also for the F.B.I. in Washington. Was this a continuation of that? Had this "accident" of getting the wrong books shown them an English angle; and had the drug-runners known it, and hit back hard?

Trivett sat patiently; waiting for Dawlish's comment.

Dawlish said softly, "Now aren't we doing well? Where did you get that from?"

"Stenway's," said Trivett promptly. "Oliver obviously was expecting trouble. He had started to write to us—either he'd just discovered the drugs in the books or else he was in trouble with the rest of the gang and was going to squeal. Several of the fake books were in his room. He hadn't hidden them—and the murderers didn't trouble to take them away."

"They may have been interrupted," Dawlish said dryly.

Trivett said, "By you?"

"Maybe." He didn't press that point.

"We're going through the lists of customers, to get on to the buyers. You told us about Oliver pretty quickly. As far as I can make out," went on Trivett, "you prevented his killers from clearing away the evidence. So we owe you something."

"Ah," said Dawlish. "And I didn't look inside a single book."

"I might believe it," said Trivett dryly.

"You can, but you needn't. What about Meyer?"

"Nothing to add," said Trivett. "Except that he's obviously in trouble, or he wouldn't have been to see you last night. You fenced with Gregg, but what have you decided to do with Meyer?"

"Help him."

"What's his trouble?"

"Off the record, he has a past. He's being blackmailed, he says. Bill, have you any idea who's behind the dope-running?"

"It could be Meyer," said Trivett, "but there's certainly nothing really to indicate that—yet. Stenway and Oliver appear to have been the big boys, and I can't yet make out why they were killed."

"Quarrel among thieves, probably," murmured Dawlish. "And someone seems to be muscling in. That's probably the answer— Stenway and Oliver were running it all nice and smoothly, the muscler-in began to muscle, and so things went wrong. And you think Uncle Zeb could be the muscler."

Trivett didn't answer.

"According to report, Homer was tracking down a dope ring, in the States, last year. Ostensibly for his newspaper, actually for the Federal Bureau of Investigation at Washington. This could be connected with that, but if it were, why did they come and lie? I think it goes farther, but that's by the way for the moment. I now have a story for you."

"I've been wondering when your conscience would get too heavy," said Trivett dryly. "Let's have it."

NINETEEN

SIMISTER

Trivett listened attentively and contrived to conceal any surprise that he felt; probably he wasn't greatly surprised. He had become used to expecting anything from Dawlish. The coffee grew cold in the pot; people came and went downstairs, but no one interrupted them. Dawlish took ten minutes longer to tell the Yard man, and when he had finished he sat back in his chair and waited for the explosion.

"I see," said Trivett mildly. "Where's the body now?"

"We took it to an empty lock-up garage in the mews—Tim has a key. No one was about."

"And what do you expect me to do? Condone the crime and forget to come and look for the body?"

Dawlish began to rub his broken nose.

"Yes," he said.

"Well, I can't. You're crazy. Why should I risk my job? My dear Pat, there are moments when you go berserk. That body was there all night, and—"

"You could let it sweat for a bit, Bill. By concealing that body I've compromised myself in the eyes of the law, as it were. Now

129

if Tim and I get rid of it, then my man of the muffled voice will probably try a little squeeze, asking me to do something else for him. I think I'd like him to start squeezing."

Trivett scowled.

"If you wanted to stick your neck out, why did you tell me about it at all? I'm a police-officer, you know."

"Someone did mention it," murmured Dawlish. "I told you because Felicity's people seem to be in trouble and there are possible international complications, and for once I thought I'd better be in the clear. Also, if I'd moved differently last night, both Corby and Oliver might be alive by now. Not a good thing to remember. So over to you, William."

Trivett said, "That won't wash. Nothing in the world would have persuaded you to tell me all this if you hadn't had a good reason. And the only good reason is that you want something else. What is it?"

"Twenty-four hours, all alone. Of course," added Dawlish, "you could come and find the body yourself and march me off to the Yard and question me and let the newspapers know about it. That's up to you. But I think you'd be wise to let it ride, while I have another go at Meyer and his little lovely. Which reminds me. Ever heard of this Dr. Simister?"

"We've heard of Simister," said Trivett, a trifle heavily. "If you mean, do we know anything against him—no, we don't. He doesn't practise in London much. He's a tuberculosis specialist, has a sanatorium in Switzerland, and comes over here every now and again. His fees hit the sky, but he's pulled off some remarkable cures."

"Why are you so dubious?" asked Dawlish.

"There have been rumours—that one or two of his patients weren't suffering from T.B. at all but had money to burn. I wouldn't like to say that it's true, but he's a money-grubber first, I'd say, and a doctor afterwards. All the same, he's clever."

"Hum," said Dawlish. "Bligh, the secretary?"

"I've been checking. Good school, Cambridge, widely travelled, until he lost most of his money about six years ago. Absolutely nothing against him."

"Rosa Meyer?"

"Now that's an interesting story," said Trivett. "It's pathetic, in its way. Rosa was in an orphanage—she's Italian by birth, her parents came over here to settle just after she was born, and died a few years later. She was lucky to get into a decent place, where they educated her well. She took up shorthand-typing, and three years ago Meyer wanted a girl; he gave her the job. She was nearly seventeen then. Soon afterwards she was taken ill, and he had her looked after. She was sent to Switzerland, and of course the only place that would be good enough for Rudolph Meyer's protégé was Simister's. I fancy Meyer was in love with the child even then. A year later he married her. On his wedding day he gave ten thousand pounds to the T.B. Research Clinic in London and the same amount to the Clinic in the United States. It's almost grotesque, for he's nearly fifty, and—well, you've seen her. But all the reports I've ever had are that they're really happy."

"What made you get the reports?" asked Dawlish.

"They crop up, over people like Meyer. You're not the only one to have become suspicious of him—we've had to screen him once or twice, but he's always come through well." Trivett looked at his watch, and whistled. "It's past twelve, I must go."

"Corby?"

"I'll see the A.C.," promised Trivett. "He may give you your twenty-four hours. At least you haven't been crazy enough to hide the body and hope for the best. What are you going to do now?"

"Go and see Meyer," said Dawlish.

* * *

Trivett still puzzled him, but Dawlish didn't dwell on that after he had left the restaurant. Outside, Tim Jeremy reported that no one had appeared to show any unusual interest in the place, and no one had followed Trivett. Tim agreed, without arguing, to go back to the flat and wait there until Felicity returned. He had just telephoned, and there had been no answer.

Dawlish's car was round a nearby corner.

He drove slowly and thoughtfully towards the West End. Rudolph Meyer's business premises were not far from his house in Larne Square. Meyer lived at Number 27.

Dawlish rang the bell, glancing round and seeing no one who appeared to take any interest in him. He watched the sun gleaming on the bonnet of his car, and he heard footsteps. A butler opened the door; Rudolph Meyer would do everything in style.

The butler, thin and elderly, took Dawlish's card upstairs. He was down again almost immediately.

"Mr. Meyer will be happy to see you, sir."

"Thanks." Dawlish beamed at him and followed him up the stairs.

Meyer was in bed, looking pale, but not as ill as he had the previous night. He held his right hand out eagerly, then pointed to a chair.

"Please sit down, my friend! I'm glad to tell you that I've had a good night, thanks largely to you. Simister will praise his drugs, of course, but my peace of mind, now that I know you are going to help all you can, is indescribable. Will you smoke?"

"Thanks," said Dawlish, accepting a cigarette.

"And I also settled my mind on another point," said Meyer. "About Bligh. He says he didn't tell me about Rosa, because he was afraid that it would upset me. He knew she had gone to see you, but took it for granted that you would let her leave before *I* arrived. Now—have you news for me?"

"I'm just probing," Dawlish said. "I wanted to know about Bligh."

"Well, *that's* explained," said Meyer. "Dawlish, I've been trying to think what can possibly be the secret of those books. It's a complete mystery to me. They were good of their kind, but not what I should call exceptional. As I told you, they originally came from my own private collection, and I sold them to Stenway. Why on earth this unknown man should want them is quite beyond me. I—ah—I know that it may be a somewhat tender subject, but it does seem rather strange that the trouble began *after* they had left this country. They reached Zebadiah Deverall in New York before Stenway was murdered. Didn't they?"

"Yes."

"I hope I don't offend you, but that *is* true. I wonder why Deverall came here?"

"So do I."

"I'm glad you are keeping an open mind on the subject," said Meyer brightly. "Well, I know you will do everything you can." He smiled. "You'll be surprised that I am so cheerful this morning, but there is a good reason. The best of reasons! Simister examined Rosa again yesterday, and telephoned me the report. She's *much* better, much better than either he or I dared hope. She's stood up to this spell in England very well indeed. He still advises that she should live permanently in Switzerland, and I shall certainly go, once this miserable business is over."

"That shouldn't take long," said Dawlish. "There was a nasty affair on the Matterhorn yesterday—did you read about it?"

Meyer looked puzzled by the change of subject.

"No. No, I haven't seen the newspapers this morning. I didn't wake up until late. Climbers killed? How sad."

If this were true, he knew nothing about Oliver's murder.

"If we could find out the secret of those books, we'd be so much farther forward, shouldn't we?" Meyer leaned back on his pillows. "It's foolish to guess, of course."

"Very," said Dawlish heavily. He leaned forward. "May I use your telephone?"

"Of course, of course!"

Dawlish asked for a personal call to Allen, at Haslemere; it came through in a few minutes.

Allen spoke.

"Hallo, Mr. Dawlish. It's about those books, I suppose."

"Yes."

"They're all fakes," said Allen. "Old Silas is quite sure of it— none of them is of any real value, and he says that it's inconceivable that a man who knows anything about old books should think that these are genuine."

Dawlish replaced the receiver slowly.

"Do you know Deverall personally?" he asked.

"No, only by reputation—and what a reputation it is! I gather there isn't a greater connoisseur of old books in the United States. Zebadiah Deverall—"

A shout outside cut across his words, made him start and break off. Dawlish swung round towards the door. There was another shout, and a crash, followed by running footsteps. A door slammed—and then a voice came clearly, with a deep American accent; an unmistakable voice.

"Let me out, or I'll break your neck."

That was Zebadiah.

TWENTY

ZEBADIAH IS ANGRY

"What—what on earth was *that*?" breathed Meyer.

"We'll have to find out, shan't we?" asked Dawlish, and moved towards the door. He glanced round as he did so, but Meyer was sitting upright on his pillows, looking pale and startled. Dawlish dropped his right hand to his pocket as he neared the door.

"Just get out of my way," roared Zebadiah.

There was another thud.

Dawlish reached the door and opened it.

Zebadiah was wearing the clothes he had worn yesterday, hair awry, unshaven, clothes rumpled, and eyes glittering, stood only a few yards away, holding a chair above his head. In front of him, and just in Dawlish's sight when he looked the other way, were the butler and another man. On the floor near them was a chair; one leg was broken.

"Just move aside," thundered Zebadiah, and looked as if he would hurl the chair.

Dawlish murmured, "Annoyed, Zeb?"

Zebadiah jumped, lowered the chair, and stared at the door. The two servants drew back, both looking scared.

"What is it, what is it?" cried Meyer.

Zebadiah tightened his grip on the chair and took a step forward.

"Who's that?" he demanded.

"Only a sick man," said Dawlish. "Fancy meeting you. Life's full of surprises, isn't it?"

"This is no time for being funny," barked Zebadiah. "Where's a telephone?"

"In here. Who do you want to call?"

"The police—who else?"

"I wouldn't know," said Dawlish. "Why?"

Zebadiah said slowly and deliberately, "Pat, I guess you've done pretty well to get here so soon, but I don't like your brand of humour. Sorry about that, but it's a fact. Who's house is this?"

"Don't you know?"

"For Pete's sake! Would I ask, if I did know?" Zebadiah looked as angry as Homer had been earlier in the day. "Would I, now?"

"I suppose not," said Dawlish. "We're in Rudolph Meyer's house."

"So we *are*," breathed Deverall. "And that was Meyer, was it? Move aside, please."

He had completely ignored the two servants, and strode towards the door. Dawlish didn't try to stop him. Zebadiah glared at the man in bed, and went slowly towards him; and he still held the chair. He stood at the foot of the bed, put the chair down slowly, and clenched his fists. The servants stood in the doorway, and Dawlish moved to one side, so that he could see both Uncle Zeb and Meyer. Meyer was frightened, and Uncle Zeb looked as fierce as an angry bull. The quiet-mannered man of the previous day had vanished. Veins stood out on his neck and his chin was thrust forward, his eyes glittered.

"So it's Meyer again," he said harshly. "You framed me, and

your gunmen brought me here. They took me down in the cellar and thought I couldn't get free. That was their mistake, Meyer, and it's yours."

Meyer's lips twisted.

"I—I—I—"

"Sure, you'll lie, but you won't expect anyone to believe you," said Uncle Zeb. "I came over here to get Stenway's killer. I put out a tempting bait, and you swallowed it. You came because of those books you thought I had with me, but I brought fakes. Understand?" His voice boomed out, and he shook a clenched fist. "Fakes, in old bindings. I knew it would fool you, and now—I want to know why you wanted those books."

"I—I don't want the books. I wish I'd never had them, I wish—"

"You *wish*," sneered Uncle Zeb. "Why, I could take your skinny neck between my fingers and choke the life out of you." He held his arms forward, the fingers crooked; and although he was two yards from Meyer, Meyer cringed back. "Talk!" roared Uncle Zeb, and rounded the bed.

As he did so there was a disturbance at the door, and Bligh appeared. He came in, set-faced, with an automatic in his right hand. He stopped at sight of Dawlish; Dawlish put his finger to his lips, to keep him quiet. Surprisingly Bligh took the hint, but moved forward so that he could see Zebadiah's face; from there he could shoot if Zebadiah started to use violence.

"I—I've nothing to say," stammered Meyer. "I know nothing about it. I've told Dawlish—"

"Dawlish may believe your lies, but I don't. Let me tell you this, Meyer. Oliver *talked*. I got to his place before your men arrived, and he *talked*. He told me that you demanded those books back. He told me that you killed Stenway because Stenway wouldn't try to get them. He told me that Corby and Bligh worked with you—"

"Bligh!" gasped Meyer. "No, no, it can't be—"

"Why don't you clear out?" Bligh asked, in an unexpectedly cool voice. "You can see Mr. Meyer's ill. You're talking out of the back of your neck. Go away."

Zebadiah didn't even look at him.

"Don't forget it, Meyer. Oliver talked. Then your hired men came, Corby and Bligh. They killed the man there, and they made me handle everything in the room. They forced me out at the point of a gun and took me to some joint which looked like an opium den. There was some trouble, and they had to take me away—know where they took me? As if you didn't know? They brought me here, to your cellar, and if you're going to pretend you know nothing about it, you're making another mistake. Dawlish might believe you, the police won't. *Why did you want those books?*"

Meyer gasped, "It's not true, Dawlish!" There was piteous entreaty in his eyes. "Dawlish, it's not true, not a word of it."

Uncle Zeb laughed.

"Go downstairs and see the cellar they kept me in, and see the ropes I managed to bite through. Go see for yourself, and then tell the police." He raised a clenched fist. "I guess that's the wrong way round. Send for the police, and then go and look."

"Ah, yes," said Dawlish mildly. "Not a bad idea."

"Bligh," sighed Meyer. "Stop this man."

Dawlish said, "Zeb, is this your Bligh?"

Zebadiah turned to look at Bligh for the first time, and shook his head impatiently.

"Bligh's a little guy, about the same size as Corby. That's not him. Are you going to send for the police, or aren't you?"

"No!" cried Rosa Meyer.

* * *

As Zebadiah flung out the question, Meyer's wife cried the word and ran forward.

"No, you can't do that, no! There's some mistake, there must be some mistake." She pushed past Zebadiah and flung herself towards Meyer. "Don't let him send for the police, don't let him!"

"All right, my pet, it's all right," whispered Meyer. "There's been a mistake."

"Mistake my eye," said Zebadiah. "Don't waste time or sympathy on your father, honey, he's not worth it. Just take her away, someone—and *Patrick*, are you going to telephone for the police?"

"No, no, no!" cried Rosa. She swung round on Dawlish. "You promised to help, you said it would be all right. Don't let them hurt Rudolph. Don't let them."

Dawlish looked into Zebadiah's eyes and found them cold and hostile. The American didn't speak, but went towards the bedside table. Rosa spread out her arms, as if she expected him to attack Meyer. Instead Zebadiah reached for the telephone.

"No!" cried Rosa.

She flung herself forward, clutched at his hand; she would have fallen, had he not gripped her arm and stopped her. He couldn't dial. Meyer watched her with horrified eyes as she crouched in front of Zebadiah, and sank slowly to her knees.

"Oh, please, no. He may have done wrong things. He may not always have been honest, but there isn't a better man living. Don't bring the police, give him a chance to explain. *Please!*"

Zebadiah looked up at Dawlish.

"I can understand why you decided to change sides," he said sardonically. "I'm not so easy. I saw Meyer's hired men kill a man."

He shook the girl's hand off his arm and started to dial; and when he finished he stared at Dawlish, as if challenging him to take any action.

Bligh moved forward.

"I don't know who you are, but you've a hell of a nerve. Put that telephone down and get out of here."

"You keep your distance," said Zebadiah levelly.

Meyer said in a hoarse voice, "I shall have to take my chance with the police, but I didn't know Deverall was here. Rosa, get up, my darling. You really mustn't upset yourself."

"That Scotland Yard?" Zebadiah asked. "This is Zebadiah Deverall—Deverall, yes. I'm at Rudolph Meyer's house, and I've some information about Oliver's murder. . . . Sure, I'll wait."

He put down the receiver.

"*Oliver's* murder?" cried Meyer. "Surely not another, not—"

"As if you didn't know," sneered Zebadiah.

Bligh launched himself at the American, fists whirling. Dawlish moved forward, quick as a flash, but Zebadiah needed no help. A crack to the jaw, one to the stomach, and an uppercut, and Bligh's feet actually left the ground before he fell.

Rosa was crying.

Two hours later Dawlish drew up in the mews. Young Gregg was near the entrance, and came to the car.

"Want me?" inquired Dawlish.

"Oh, no! What an idea! I'm just keeping an eye on your American guests," said Gregg. "We don't want to take any risks with them, do we?"

Dawlish smiled sceptically.

He glanced at the window, and saw Felicity's face pressed against the window. Then she disappeared inside, and the door opened as he reached the top of the steps. Elvira was behind her. He didn't worry about Elvira, but hugged Felicity and kissed her.

"Safe, Pat?"

"Oh, no! Half-dead. Look at me. I am officially informed that it's all over. Meyer and two of his servants have been charged with abducting the person of Zebadiah Deverall, citizen of the United States, and they'll be held in custody. Rosa's prostrate. Simister says that it will take her weeks to get over this, and it might set her right back where she started. I don't know how true that is, but she wasn't looking so good. Hallo, Elvira. Nice, slow-moving, sleepy place you've come to."

"Hallo, Pat," Elvira said slowly. "Where's Dad?"

"At the Embassy. I have also been to the Embassy. I am not so popular as I was. Zeb's let them know that I was engaged by both sides, and he doesn't think much of it. Why are you behaving so oddly, Elvira? What do you know?"

Homer appeared in the doorway.

"Don't answer, sis." His eyes had a nasty look, and his lips were drawn tightly; it gave the impression that his mouth was cruel. "We'll wait for Dad, and then we'll get out. I'm not surprised Patrick worked on both sides."

"Oh, be quiet!" snapped Elvira. "I don't care what Dad or you say. *I* don't think Pat would double-cross us. Pat, did you think Meyer was the man behind the trouble? Were you double-crossing *him*?"

Dawlish shook his head.

"No, I wasn't double-crossing Meyer," he said. "I don't think Meyer's guilty. Fel, you've a queer bunch of relatives, and although you'll hate to hear me say so, my favourite is Elvira."

The telephone bell rang, and at the same time a car drew up outside. Elvira moved quickly across to the window.

"It's Dad," she said, and ran into the hall.

"Dawlish speaking," said Dawlish into the telephone.

"Hold on, please, Mr. Dawlish. Mr. Trivett is calling you."

Dawlish stretched out his legs. Elvira opened the front door and ran down the steps, and Zebadiah's deep, pleasing voice sounded delighted. Homer stirred restlessly but watched Dawlish.

Trivett came on the line.

"Hallo, Pat. It's all finished—I thought you'd like to know."

"Really?" asked Dawlish politely.

"And don't use that tone of voice. It was Meyer. He was the king pin of a smuggling and dope-peddling racket that was worldwide. Bligh's talked—he's had his suspicions for some time. He tried to lie for Meyer's sake, but admits that Corby and another Bligh—his own brother—were in with Meyer. Rosa knew, too. She'd sell her soul for Rudolph, but she doesn't know the tricks, and she's let a lot out. I know you weren't sure of Meyer, so I thought I'd let you know."

Dawlish drew a deep breath.

"You still there?" Trivett demanded sharply.

"Oh, yes," said Dawlish, still politely. "Nice of you. Only I don't believe it. Good-bye."

TWENTY-ONE

FRIEND IN NEED

As Dawlish replaced the receiver Zebadiah came into the room. He smiled at Felicity as he strolled across to Dawlish, and Elvira drew away.

"Well, Patrick," he said. "What don't you believe?"

"That we have the right villains," said Dawlish.

"So you're still putting your money on Meyer?"

"Some of it."

"You're wrong," said Zebadiah firmly, but there was no annoyance in his voice or his expression. "I guess that needn't prevent us from being good friends. I owe you an apology, Pat, and I hope you'll accept it."

"Oh, lor'. None due!"

"There is, Pat. I was pretty angry at Meyer's house. I'd been in that cellar all night and hadn't eaten for a long time. Was I mad at anyone who ran into me! I suggested that you were working on both sides, and that was an insult which I'm happy to withdraw. Think you would have found me in that cellar?"

"I doubt it. Still, I've been lucky in the past," said Dawlish. "Who knows?"

"I guess it's of no importance any more." Zebadiah smiled broadly. "You can hold your opinion about Meyer as long as you like, Pat, but I don't feel there's any more danger for me or for Elvira. Or for Homer, if it comes to that. Supposing we forget all about it? We've only a day or two left, will you show us round?"

"Pat, please do that!" Elvira was eager.

"How long have you?" asked Dawlish.

"We ought to be getting back soon. I'm booking for the day after tomorrow."

"Stay two more days, and I'll show you the town."

"Oh, do that, Dad!"

"It's kind of difficult," frowned Zebadiah.

"You can manage *two* more days," Elvira said. "You just have to do it."

"What do you say, son?" asked Zebadiah.

"Suits me," said Homer.

"Then we'll agree on that, Pat," said Zebadiah. "No bad feeling, I hope?"

"My dear Zeb! Why on earth should there be? I'll get the guide-books out and telephone a few friends of mine and show you the best and the worst I can, tomorrow. I've several things I must do today. Must recover some of my lost prestige. But that needn't stop you looking round. I'll be back."

He waved a hand to include everyone, and hurried out. Felicity followed him, but he was on the steps before she reached the hall, beckoning Gregg. She went down the steps as Gregg came up.

"No trouble, is there?" Gregg looked alarmed.

"Oh, not a bit. Tell me, as man to man—are you watching me or the citizens of the United States?"

"I've told you."

"Orders to follow them wherever they go?"

"The young couple," said Gregg.

"Fine! Any reason why you shouldn't go with them, as one of the party?"

Gregg looked puzzled.

"I suppose not, but—"

"Fine! They want to go sight-seeing, and who could do the East End better than a Yard man? Limehouse, Wapping, and all the places of infamy that people imagine they'll find in London. I can't take them round today, and I'd be much happier if you were with them."

"I'll have to ask Mr. Trivett," said Gregg dubiously.

"Come in and use the telephone," invited Dawlish.

At half-past three the Deveralls and Gregg left the flat. Gregg led the way, with Elvira by his side. Dawlish and Felicity stood at the window and watched—and Dawlish looked mournful as he said:

"I don't think she'll want to borrow me, after all."

"You didn't expect that nonsense would last long, did you? Pat, what's on your mind? Why did you act that way? Are you sure Trivett's wrong?"

"Oh, yes," said Dawlish. "I think he knows he hasn't got everything yet, too. He's prodding me, to see how far I'll go. Where's Tim?"

"In the dining-room, dozing."

Dawlish chuckled.

"He won't have much more time to doze! My sweet, I'm going over to see Bill Farningham, so I'll be at the hospital if I'm wanted in the next hour. 'Bye."

Bill Farningham had once been a member of a foursome which had earned something of a reputation in a great variety of circles. When Dawlish had first been involved in crime, Tim Jeremy, Ted Beresford, and Farningham had been with him; and on occasions they forgathered and decided that nothing would ever be quite the same as that first wild adventure. Bill had since settled down to a contented marriage, children, and his medical career. After a few years at St. Mede's Hospital he had gone into private practice, but had sold the practice, and was now the House Physician at St. Mede's, which was on the south side of the Thames, near Lambeth Bridge.

Dawlish, making sure that he was not followed, reached the hospital at a quarter-past four. The receptionist regretted that it was impossible to see Dr. Farningham without an appointment, but was prevailed upon to send up Dawlish's card. Two minutes later Farningham came hurrying in.

"Pat, you old sinner! How are you?"

"Ill," said Dawlish sorrowfully. "Terrible. You'd never believe. Can I have a quick diagnosis?"

Farningham chuckled.

"Come upstairs, and I'll put you through it."

In his office he settled Dawlish in an easy-chair and said:

"Now, what's the trouble?"

Dawlish looked forlorn.

"I think I have T.B."

"If that's a joke, it's in bad taste."

"But I might want to go to Switzerland."

Farningham looked almost alarmed.

"What's it all about?"

"If I had T.B. I should be better off in Switzerland, shouldn't I?"

"Not necessarily. If it were pulmonary, yes, of course."

"How soon could you tell if I had it?"

"How badly would you have it?" asked Farningham mildly.

Dawlish grinned. "I wondered how long you'd be twigging

it. Well, badly. I should have been in Switzerland—at a famous sanatorium—for two or three different spells. I should have been discharged as cured, once, but it was all a mistake. I'm in England now, seeing if I can stand the climate, but I'll almost certainly be on my way back to Switzerland before the end of the summer."

"Summer's over. I could tell you, in a case like that, in a few hours. As long as it takes to have an X-ray done and the plate developed."

"Supposing I were unconscious. I mean, drugged by some harmless drug that made me sleepy. Could you examine me while I was unconscious, and give a definite opinion?"

"Yes. It's much better for the patient to be conscious, but this could be done."

"Wonderful! The girl I have in mind—"

"Well, well! Does Felicity know her?"

"She knows about her. She—the girl—might possibly have been fooled. So might her husband. A certain Dr. Simister is concerned."

Farningham looked down his nose.

"It could be done. I'd want to screen her lungs, find out if there were any healed lesions. Would she have to be unconscious all the time?"

"She wouldn't have to know that she was being medically examined, if that's what you mean."

"That's what I mean," said Farningham. "Well, the best drug would be thiopentone. It's quite safe. It would have to be injected, and repeated once or twice, but it doesn't affect the patient much."

"And what should be used to put her off to sleep quickly in the first place? Before the injection—she might possibly object to an injection. Something that could be put in a chocolate, say."

Farningham hesitated.

"Nembutal, probably—but it would take some time to put her off. Probably half an hour."

"Make it less, if you can. And give me the stuff so that I can put it in a chocolate."

"I suppose I'd better," said Farningham.

"It's vital. If I brought an unconscious patient in, told you that I suspected T.B. and all that kind of thing, you could give me a pretty clear idea twelve hours or so afterwards."

"Yes," said Farningham. "I ought to have some knowledge of the case history."

"I might be able to get that, but might draw a blank. Is it essential?"

"No," said Farningham.

An hour later Dawlish sprawled back in his easy-chair, with Tim opposite him and Felicity on a pouffe. All was quiet. Since he had returned Tim had told him that Corby's body had been removed and that Felicity now knew about that incident. Felicity made no comment, and with Tim she watched Dawlish patiently.

"Well, what are we going to do?" asked Tim.

Dawlish opened one eye.

"Pat, why *are* you going on with it? Everyone seems satisfied."

Dawlish opened the other eye.

"Except Meyer and his Rosa," he said. "Oh, I could be wrong, but I think little Rudolph has had a raw deal. This is one of the foulest cases that we've come up against—worldwide marihuana distribution. If we've got everyone concerned, fine. If we haven't, if it can be continued after Meyer's gaoled—or hanged—then we're where we started. All over the world, there are human beings falling for their pipe-dreams, losing their self-control, gradually succumbing to the dope which turns them into beasts. Aren't I getting emotional? Dope rots 'em, body and soul. I'd like to try to make sure the rot's stopped."

The softness of his voice gave the words vehemence.

After a pause Felicity said, "All right, Pat."

"It shouldn't take long. All we have to do is break into Dr. Simister's consulting-rooms and find his case-history of Rosa Meyer. After that, all we have to do is kidnap Rosa. Bligh's looking after her, so there isn't much to beat. Easy!"

Tim began to smile.

"And where are you going to keep Rosa?" asked Felicity. "Here?"

"Oh, no. Patient, under a false name, at St. Mede's. It's all laid on with Bill. And if we find that she hasn't T.B. and that Simister has been playing Meyer for a sucker, squeezing thousands of pounds out of him for services which weren't required, making hell on earth for him and his wife, then we can tell ourselves that Meyer might not be guilty of the other business, after all—that Simister might be involved. Bligh, too—my money's on Bligh— and others we don't yet know. Worth the gamble?"

Felicity nodded.

"When do we start?"

"After dark tonight," said Dawlish. "With luck, we'll have both jobs done before breakfast. And tomorrow we go sight-seeing. I'll show young Gregg how to deal with Americans."

"You won't go alone," said Felicity coldly.

TWENTY-TWO

CASE-HISTORY

The wind, which had quietened during the day, sprang up again that night and swept along Wimpole Street, whistling round the corner. Dawlish and Tim reached Number 88a, a house in a long terrace, with half a dozen brass plates fastened to the wall. No light shone from the fanlight over the door or from the windows.

Dawlish stood on the porch, by the door, and Tim on the pavement. Both wore thin gloves. A taxi passed, and then silence followed.

"Right," whispered Tim.

Dawlish set to work on the Yale lock with a piece of mica. His hands were quite steady. The risks here were greater than at Stenway's bookshop, but his mood was different.

"Steady," Tim called.

A car swept along the street, its headlights on. Dawlish dropped his hand from the lock, and looked as if he were waiting for the door to open. The car drew nearer, and the light showed up the names on the brass plates, including that of R. D. Simister, M.D., F.R.C.P. The car passed, and Dawlish started again.

The lock clicked back.

"Right," he whispered, and stepped inside. Tim followed him, and they closed the door, although it wouldn't latch properly now. Dawlish pushed it as far as it would go, and then switched on a torch, and Tim fetched an upright chair and placed it against the door.

They moved away, the beam of light carving a white line through the darkness, shining on doors and chairs; there was a faint smell of antiseptics.

"Know what floor?" Tim asked.

"One flight up."

"Here we go!"

They found the stairs, and then Dawlish put out the light and led the way up. Once the headlights of a car outside shone through a landing-window, and cast ghostly shadows which moved before they faded.

They reached the landing.

"We can use a bit more light here," said Tim.

Dawlish turned the head of his torch, and when he pressed the switch a diffused glow spread about them, not the powerful white beam. There were doors and two passages; and there was no name on any of the doors.

"But they're all locked," Tim said gloomily.

Each door was.

Dawlish took out a key-case; on it was a skeleton key. It seemed lost in his great hand, but he moved it deftly; the first lock was forced in less than a minute.

They stepped into a large room, and the glow spread round. It shone on photographs of two children and a woman. Dawlish went to the books on a small desk, picked one up and glanced at the flyleaf. He read: "P. M. Gregory".

"No go."

Tim looked gloomier.

They went into two other rooms, locking the doors after them, before they found Simister's. His name was on several books, but they didn't need that; a photograph of the specialist himself was on the mantelpiece; smiling and smug.

"Now we're moving." Tim stepped to filing-cabinets at one side of the room. There were three. He opened the first, Dawlish the second, and they found files, the dossiers, or case-histories of the patients. "Not mine," said Tim. "I'm R to Z."

"I start at G," said Dawlish, and Tim shifted the light, so that he could see more clearly. "Masters—Medway—Mellish—Merlin—ah!"

He drew out a manilla folder, with several papers inside. There were three cards, filled with hieroglyphics; even words which he knew to be written in non-medical language were practically unreadable, but on each card Rosa Meyer's name was typed at the top. There were several X-ray photographs and reports.

"It looks pretty comprehensive."

He wished it didn't.

"Look at another, see how it compares," suggested Tim.

Dawlish opened another folder. The contents were almost identical with Rosa's, except that there were fewer entries.

Dawlish put the second file back, tucked Rosa's under his arm, and closed the drawer.

"Not so good," murmured Tim.

"Why not?"

"Would he put down a lot of notes if it was a fake case-history?"

"I don't know," said Dawlish. "I'd say he probably would. He isn't the only one with access to the records. He must have a secretary and probably changes them from time to time. He'd want to be sure that if he has any faked case-records it couldn't be seen by anyone who knew anything about the disease."

"I suppose not." Tim was sceptical.

Dawlish creased the folder so that it would go in his inside coat pocket, and turned away from the cabinets.

"Not going to have a look round for anything else?"

"I don't think so," said Dawlish. "I can't imagine he would leave anything else here that might do him harm. The quicker we're out, the better. What's the time?"

"Twenty-five past nine."

"Little Rosa will be in bed if we don't hurry," said Dawlish.

He re-locked the door, and they went downstairs in the light of the torch, switching it off when they reached the hall. They left the building, with the door slightly open; there was nothing they could do about that. They walked briskly along to Dawlish's car, and Dawlish took the wheel.

"Straight to Rosa?" asked Tim.

"I think so—and you'll have half an hour to spare. Will you take the case-history to the hospital, have it sealed up for Bill, leave it, and be at Meyer's place as soon as you can?"

"Right."

The tall, elderly butler opened the door at Meyer's house, peered at Dawlish short-sightedly, and then drew back. He looked frail and his hands were trembling a little as he waited for Dawlish to speak.

"Good—good evening, sir."

"Is Mrs. Meyer in?"

"Well, sir—"

"This is urgent," Dawlish said.

"I see, sir, but—she is in her room. The doctor ordered her to stay in her room for two or three days, and said that she wasn't to see anyone. That has happened before, and she has had such a terrible time that I shouldn't like to do anything which might make her worse."

"Of course not," Dawlish said. He stood in the hall, and the butler closed the door. "Tell her I'm here, will you, and tell her I think I shall have good news soon."

"*Good* news?" The butler's eyes blazed. "Of Mr. Meyer?"

"Yes."

"But—but I thought you—you were on the side of the police, Mr. Dawlish!"

"Only of the innocent."

"Mr. Dawlish," said the butler hoarsely, "if there is anything I can do to help Mr. Meyer, please tell me. I have served him for over four years, and—and I have never known a kinder or more generous man. *All* the staff would do anything to help him. And if you could get him free, we—we should always be grateful."

There were actually tears in the man's eyes.

"If it's possible it'll be done," said Dawlish gently. "I shouldn't worry too much. Will you tell Mrs. Meyer that I'm here?"

"Of course—of course, sir. I won't keep you many minutes. Will you wait in here?"

He started towards a door on the right.

"This will do me," said Dawlish.

"Very well."

The butler hurried towards the stairs, footsteps muffled by the thick carpet. By the time he had disappeared from sight, there was silence—and it was almost profound. Dawlish glanced about him casually, went to an old oak settle, sat down, and lit a cigarette. As he put his lighter away, he glanced at a door opposite. It didn't move; but he thought it had, soon after he had arrived.

He stood up, and turned his back.

When he looked round again, the door was wider open; not much, but sufficient to convince him that someone had heard him come, and didn't yet want him to know it. He whistled softly. There was no light on in the room.

He strolled across to the door casually. The door was still, now, and he could hear no sound. He had a box of chocolates under his arm; very special chocolates.

The butler came hurrying.

"Mrs. Meyer will be happy to see you, sir."

The butler led the way upstairs, Dawlish followed, wondering about the moving door. Had it been the wind? He doubted it, but couldn't be sure. Bligh? If it were Bligh, why had he not made himself known? It was unlikely that Bligh would want him to see Rosa. Dawlish was half-way up when he heard a door open below. He didn't look round, until Bligh said in a harsh voice:

"Martin! Where are you going?"

The butler started, and turned round. Dawlish also turned to see Bligh coming towards the stairs, brisk and alert, very good-looking in the soft light of the hall.

"Mr. Dawlish is going to see Mrs. Meyer, sir. I've seen her, and she feels quite well enough."

"Well, she isn't well enough," said Bligh. He hurried up the stairs, but Dawlish blocked his way, and he had to stand two steps down. "Dr. Simister said that she mustn't be excited in any way. You ought to have known better than to send his name up." Bligh was severe. "Sorry, Dawlish."

"Don't be sorry," murmured Dawlish. "No need. I couldn't disappoint her now."

Bligh said thinly, "Mr. Meyer isn't here, and Mrs. Meyer is a sick woman. I am in charge, and I refuse to let you go to see her without first consulting Dr. Simister."

"Oh. Is he here?"

"He is not, and won't be until tomorrow afternoon. If you have anything to talk to Mrs. Meyer about, it will have to wait until then."

"Pity," said Dawlish. "I hate defying the man of the house, but it can't be helped."

He turned round.

Bligh said, "Martin, you are not to show Mr. Dawlish the way."

"Certainly not," said Dawlish. "It wouldn't do to disobey orders. I'll find my own way, Martin, thanks."

He pushed past the butler and reached the landing—and wasn't sure, even when he reached it, that Bligh had given up the fight.

TWENTY-THREE

CHOCOLATES

Bligh hadn't given up. He pushed Martin roughly against the wall, passed him, and reached the landing as Dawlish pushed open the door of a room which was already ajar. He put a hand on Dawlish's arm, and said angrily:

"What the hell do you think you're doing?"

"Looking for Mrs. Meyer."

"Get out."

"Haven't I made myself clear yet?" asked Dawlish mildly. "Let me repeat it. I'm going to see Mrs. Meyer, and all the Blighs and all the Simisters in England aren't going to keep me away. Good evening."

"If she has a relapse, the responsibility will be yours."

"Oh, yes. As Mr. Meyer was in bed last night, and Mrs. Meyer was ill, you were responsible for what happened then, weren't you? Such as having men locked up in the cellar."

"I knew nothing about that. The *police* are quite satisfied about my innocence. Dawlish—"

"Sorry. I'm just naturally obstinate."

Bligh said softly, "Dawlish, I'm telling you not to go into Mrs.

Meyer's room, understand? She mustn't be excited. She has had a terrible time, and you will only make it worse. If I can take her a message—"

"Oh, no. Private consultation."

Bligh swung round, went farther along a wide passage and reached a door on the right. He obviously thought that he was there ahead of Dawlish, glanced round, and was startled to see Dawlish at his side, beaming fatuously. He pushed the door open with a perfunctory tap, and strode inside; he would have closed the door, but for Dawlish's foot, which got in the way.

Rosa Meyer was standing in front of a writing-table; this was a sitting-room, small, delightfully furnished. A door, standing ajar, obviously led to the bedroom. She was smiling in anticipation at first, then frowned when she saw Bligh.

"Why, Gerald—"

"Rosa, you are not to talk to Mr. Dawlish. Dr. Simister was most emphatic that you mustn't have visitors."

"But Gerald—"

"Sorry. It can't be helped."

"Sorry," echoed Dawlish. "Nor can this."

He gripped Bligh's right arm, and twisted it slightly; Bligh was forced into a position from which he couldn't move. His mouth was slightly open, as if in astonishment. Dawlish pushed him out of the room, closed the door firmly, and turned the key in the lock. He left the key where it was, and turned to Rosa, who was staring at him—astonished, but not appalled.

"Hallo," said Dawlish brightly. "Don't worry about Gerald Bligh, he's only doing his best. A poor best, I'm afraid."

"He—he'll be furious!"

"People do get furious with me," said Dawlish sadly. "Love or hate, you know the kind of thing. Don't worry about him."

She looked at the door, then went to a chair and sat down

slowly. She looked—superb. Her colour was just right and her complexion perfect. She wore a red house-coat, done up high at the neck and cut subtly, to show the lines of her figure; her figure wasn't girlish, by any means; he hadn't noticed that so much the previous night.

He sat opposite her, and put the box of chocolates on a table near her.

"I thought they might cheer you up. There's a special kind in them—really special liqueurs."

She glanced at them.

"You're very good. But—nothing will cheer me up, I'm afraid, until I've good news of Rudolph. I can hardly believe that it's really happened, even now. It *is* true that he sometimes saw this man Corby and Gerald's brother. And we *knew* Gerald's brother was a bad lot, Gerald's often warned Rudolph against him. But—I didn't dream it would be anything like this. I'm so worried, I'm almost out of my mind. The police asked *hundreds* of questions. I wanted to protect Rudolph, but before I'd finished I hardly knew what I was saying. Do you think I've—harmed him?"

Dawlish smiled.

"Did you tell the truth?"

"Of course!"

"It never did anyone any harm with the police to tell the truth," said Dawlish. "Relax, Mrs. Meyer. Have a chocolate!"

He chuckled and leaned back, massive and reassuring; and he thought that he had already helped to calm her.

She took the box and began to pick at the cellophane wrapping.

"What can I do to help Rudolph?"

"Tell me what you told the police," said Dawlish. "There's one big difference—they think that the evidence is strong against Rudolph. I'm not sure. I think there's a loop-hole, and we'll find it."

She pulled the wrapping-paper off and opened the box absently.

"There are the specials," Dawlish said. Three were on top, treated with nembutal, and wrapped in silver paper. "The silvery ones."

"Well—I hardly remember what I did tell them." Rosa didn't take one. "How often Rudolph saw Corby and Gerald's brother, that was one thing. And that he was often away from home. Nothing that really makes him look a criminal, and—I didn't tell a thing about his past. Not a thing! I was terrified in case I should, but they didn't ask anything about that, and thank God I was able to keep quiet."

"Wonderful," said Dawlish.

She held out the box.

"Will you—have one?"

Dawlish took a chocolate wrapped in green foil. She hesitated—then took a doctored one. Dawlish watched her put it into her mouth, and felt a great relief. She didn't speak for a few moments, but watched him closely.

"Did they ask you if he had ever seen Zebadiah Deverall here?"

"Oh, yes! He hadn't, as far as I knew."

"Elvira Deverall?"

"No, they didn't inquire much about her," said Rosa, "but they asked many questions about *Homer* Deverall. He's never been here, as far as I know, and I've certainly never seen him before."

"Have you seen him now?"

"Only a photograph," said Rosa. "I should think it was a very good one. I couldn't understand why they asked all those questions about the Americans. I could understand them asking about Stenway and Oliver, and—and that seemed to please the police most. Of course, Rudolph did a lot of business with Stenway's, and saw both men frequently. They often came here. Why, Stenway occasionally flew out to Switzerland, to see Rudolph; the business was often as urgent as that. It was *only* business."

She was so young and earnest.

"Of course," said Dawlish. "And who else were they interested in?"

"No one," said Rosa, and added tremulously, "except me. Oh, and Gerald, of course. They asked a few questions about him."

She broke off, and coughed. It wasn't much of a cough, but now it had started, it kept on. Dawlish had heard coughing like that before—in friends whom, he knew, were suffering from tuberculosis. It didn't seem to distress her much. She talked freely, mostly about the police interviews, ate two more chocolates, and began to yawn.

Soon, her eyelids were drooping, she could hardly keep awake.

Dawlish stood up.

"I've tired you," he said apologetically. "I should go to bed if I were you, Mrs. Meyer. And remember that I shall do everything I can to help Rudolph."

"You're so—very good." She yawned again, and stood up slowly. Her eyes looked heavy, and she was obviously puzzled. "I can't understand it, I'm not often as tired as this. Will you—will you ring that bell for me?"

She pointed to a bell by the fire-place.

"Can I help?"

"Oh, no, Mrs. Harris will come up, that's all. Our housekeeper," said Rosa, and yawned again. "I'll go and lie down until she comes." She forced a smile. "Good night."

Dawlish went to the bell and pretended to push; he didn't.

Rosa went through the doorway which was partly open, and a moment later heard a faint sound. He stepped towards the door, and peered through the crack between the wall and the door, but saw nothing. Yet a light was on. He straightened up—and saw the lighted room and then realized what was blocking his way.

Bligh was behind the door.

Dawlish went across to the writing-table, and picked up the two remaining doctored chocolates. Bligh was probably already suspicious, and was the only obstacle to full success. Bligh was probably looking at him, now. He went to the door, stepped out, closed the door, and made for the stairs. He didn't go down, but slipped into another room. A minute later, Bligh came out of the girl's bedroom; there was another door to it, from the landing. Dawlish couldn't see his face clearly, but thought that he was frowning.

Bligh went into a room across the landing.

Dawlish slipped out, went to Rosa's room, and saw what he wanted—her hand-bag, on the dressing-table. She was fast asleep, still wearing the house-coat, but her slippers were off and her small, white feet and ankles showed, delicate as alabaster. Bligh hadn't troubled to try to cover her up. Dawlish opened the bag, and took out the keys, slipped them into his pocket, and went out again.

He heard a voice.

As he drew near the room where Bligh had gone, he recognized Bligh's voice.

". . . and she dropped asleep while he was talking to her. He brought her some chocolates, as I told you. I don't get it, but I wouldn't like to trust him. . . . What do you recommend?"

Dawlish leaned against the wall, and wondered what Dr. Simister would recommend; there wasn't much doubt, in his mind, that Bligh was talking to the specialist.

"All right, I'll expect you in an hour," said Bligh. "I'll just watch her, until then. I wish I could think why he wanted her asleep. . . . Okay, Simmy."

He rang off.

Dawlish smiled in the half-light of the landing. Bligh didn't move, for a few moments. No one else was up here, and Dawlish could see over the banisters to the hall; Martin wasn't in sight down there. Tim was waiting outside, by now, and in an hour the doctor would be here. Meanwhile Bligh would watch Rosa so closely that the only way to get her out of the house would be by fighting his way past a bodyguard. He didn't fancy that just now.

Bligh moved towards the door, and his shadow appeared. His head was lowered, chin on chest. He didn't glance right, towards Dawlish, but turned to the girl's bedroom. He obviously didn't hear a sound as Dawlish went after him, moved his great arms, and gripped Bligh round the neck. Bligh gave a choking sound, went limp, and tried to twist his head round; he couldn't. Dawlish increased the pressure. Bligh back-heeled, and caught Dawlish painfully on the shin, but Dawlish's grip didn't relax. Bligh waved his arms wildly, kicked again less painfully, and tried desperately to turn his head. He didn't try for long, but went limp; all his weight leaned against Dawlish.

Dawlish released him, cautiously. The man wasn't foxing, but was unconscious and would be out for ten minutes or more. Dawlish carried him back into the room from which he had telephoned; a beautifully appointed study. He sat him in an easy-chair, then went to the window, cut the cords off the blinds and used them to tie Bligh's feet and wrists. He stuffed a handkerchief into the man's mouth, and, satisfied that there was no danger from Bligh in the immediate future, went back to the landing.

He thought he heard movement, glanced over the landing, and saw Martin standing in the middle of the hall and looking up. Martin sighed and shook his head, and then went out of sight.

Was he now in another room? The servants' quarters? Or was he in another part of the hall, waiting for Dawlish to leave so that he could speak to him as he went out?

Dawlish stepped forward, and hurried down the stairs. Martin came from a recess in the hall, eagerly.

"How is she, sir?"

"Tired out," said Dawlish. "She asked Mrs. Harris to go up in half an hour—not sooner. And I'll try to bring good news in the morning. All the household in, now?"

"Yes, sir."

"You can lock up and go to bed, then."

"Thank you, sir, I will go to bed, but Mr. Bligh always locks up."

"Good."

Dawlish smiled, the more warmly because the front door wouldn't be locked and bolted against him.

Martin saw him to the door, waited as he turned out of sight, then went in and closed the door. Tim appeared from the wheel of his car, twenty yards away; an eager Tim.

"How did it go?"

"Fair. It's now or never, Tim. We'll give the butler a couple of minutes, and then—"

Dawlish stopped, for a car turned into the square, and he recognized it beneath the light of a street lamp. He not only recognized the car, but the driver. His eyes narrowed as the car came up.

"What—" began Tim, turned, and groaned. "*Trivett!*"

* * *

Dawlish thrust the keys into Tim's hand, and whispered urgently:

"Go in, upstairs, third door on the right. You'll find Rosa fast asleep and reasonably respectable. Put a blanket or something over her, bring her out, and take her straight to St. Mede's. Bill Farningham will be waiting. He has it all laid on. I'll stall Trivett, somehow."

"Right!"

Trivett's car pulled up, and without getting out, he looked at them from the window; the light was good enough to show his broad smile. He was alone; at least Dawlish was getting some kind of a break.

"Well, well, the conspirators themselves! Have you just arrived, or are you leaving?"

"Leaving," said Dawlish. "Tim, you go and tell Felicity I'll be late, will you? Use my car. Don't get out, Bill, I've a lot to say, and you'd better hear it before you see Bligh or Mrs. Meyer. Spare ten minutes?"

"Get in," said Trivett.

Dawlish hurried round to the other side of the car. As he settled down, Trivett switched off the engine.

"Not here," Dawlish said urgently. "Bligh might look out of a window, and I don't want him to know that we're in a huddle. Round the corner will do."

Trivett might agree, without protest; or might laugh and call the idea nonsense.

TWENTY-FOUR

TRIVETT OBLIGES

Trivett laughed, switched on the engine, and drove to the nearest corner. He pulled up twenty yards along the street, between two lamps, and as he switched off the engine, glanced sideways at Dawlish, and said dryly:

"It's nice and dark here, now we shan't be recognizable. Afraid of being shot?"

"Yes." Dawlish was abrupt.

He thought he saw Trivett frown, and there was no doubt about the change in the tone of the Yard man's voice.

"Are you fooling?"

"No. Bill, you're so sure you're right about Meyer, and it's going to lead to a lot of trouble. I'm not sure, and that means that they're going to do anything to stop me from finding out the truth—especially now. You don't need telling they are killers, and that if you've the wrong man in Meyer, some of the killers are still at large."

Trivett was brusque.

"Yes." He paused. "Why especially now?"

"I've had a talk with Rosa Meyer. Bligh did his damnedest to prevent it. As he failed, he's been in a huddle with Dr. Simister."

"What's surprising?" asked Trivett. "Simister says she must rest. I've undertaken not to question her again today. Bligh probably had orders to keep anyone from her."

"Oh, it looks all right on the surface," said Dawlish. "Bill, are you really as sure as you say you are? Or have you something up your sleeve? You've soft-pedalled with me, let me get away with the Corby business—which means that the A.C. approved—and you've put Gregg up as an Aunt Sally, dogging me as much as you could. Why?"

Trivett said slowly, "Because from the beginning I knew what was behind this business. I suspected that Stenway and Oliver were dope trafficking on a world-wide scale. I wanted to get at the big shot behind them. It's been on such a big scale that I wanted you to have your head—you blunder on to a lot of things that we don't discover." Trivett smiled faintly in the gloom. "If blunder's the word! There was another thing; I knew that Homer Deverall had been working on the dope business from the New York angle. He represents a newspaper, but is also an F.B.I. man. That's established."

"Well, well!"

"I can tell you something else," said Trivett. "Your Uncle Zebadiah had a book in a shipment from Stenway which contained drugs. Homer opened the parcel, which was sent by post and wasn't opened by Customs. Homer and his father decided to report it to the New York Police. The police pretended to take little or no notice of it, but actually they worked at high pressure. The reason for Meyer's attempt to throw a scare into Zebadiah seems obvious—he wanted to find out if the police knew about that book, and wanted the book. Another thing—Stenway was killed because he made that slip. We've caught the other Bligh, Thomas Bligh—as nasty a piece of work as we've ever come across. Anything we needed in the way of evidence against Meyer, we can get. This is one of your mistakes, Pat."

Dawlish said slowly, "I'm beginning to believe it. But Stenway wasn't killed simply because he sent out a book of the drugs in mistake. It's almost incredible that he should make a mistake of that kind, anyhow."

"Even you make 'em, at times!" Trivett was almost smug. "Actually, Stenway slipped up, Meyer lost his temper with him, threatened to cut him out of the ring. Stenway turned nasty and said if that happened, he'd shop the whole gang. So Meyer played safe, and had him killed. Corby and Thomas Bligh did the job."

"Did Thomas Bligh get orders from Meyer himself?"

"Corby took the orders. Thomas Bligh's come across with all this because he knows the only thing to save him is turning King's Evidence. He's an accessory to both the murders, but says Corby actually committed them. He doesn't know who killed Corby. We'll find out. Pat, I don't know why you think you've a special reason to feel nervous now, but you haven't. It's finished."

"I see," said Dawlish. "Why come here at this time of night, then?"

"I've a statement for Gerald Bligh to sign. He didn't want to leave the house again, because he has to look after Mrs. Meyer, so I brought it round."

"So you're spoon-feeding Gerald Bligh," murmured Dawlish. "Well, I suppose I can't blame you. Take him the statement by all means. On the other hand, you could be advised by me, just for once. I don't often ask favours—"

Trivett burst out laughing.

"All right, all right," growled Dawlish. "Not this kind. Give Bligh a miss tonight. Have the house watched and Bligh followed, if you like, or better still, wait until the morning before you see Bligh. You may find you've reason to believe he's up to the neck in it, and that Meyer's innocent."

Trivett considered for a long time. Dawlish didn't know for certain, but Tim was almost certainly on the way to St. Mede's. Gerald Bligh probably hadn't been found.

"Pat, you're as stubborn as a mule, and I can't say I blame you, but give it up, this time. Go and take the Deverall family out. I'm taking the watch off them tonight. Gregg's had a good enough time. He—" Trivett broke off and snapped his fingers. "The young devil!" he breathed.

"Now what's he done?"

"I told him to finish tonight, and he asked if he could take a couple of days' leave that's due to him. If he's going to continue as a guide to London, I'll have the pants off him!"

"If I know Elvira," said Dawlish, "you can get ready for his pants. Well, please yourself, Bill. Go and get Bligh to sign on the dotted line, and see what happens afterwards. If I can prove he's lying, and he's signed a false statement, it might help to damn him. So go ahead."

Trivett started the engine.

"I'll give you twelve hours," he said finally. "Say until noon tomorrow."

Dawlish flashed, "Make it four in the afternoon."

He concealed his grin of delight, that Trivett was going to give Meyer's house a miss. He wouldn't run into a Bligh who was bound and gagged, and jump to the right conclusion.

"You're pretty confident over this," mused Trivett. "You almost make me think someone else is concerned. All right—four o'clock."

"I'll come to the Yard for tea," promised Dawlish.

"Do. Anywhere I can drop you?"

"Tim's flat, if it's all right with you," said Dawlish. "Did I ever tell you you're the wisest policeman I know?"

Trivett laughed.

Dawlish heard singing as he stepped into the mews, looked up, and saw a shadowy figure outlined against the window. A man's. Trivett had already driven off; he might, by now, have news on the way that Bligh had been attacked, if Bligh were confident enough to report the assault to the police. Dawlish doubted whether he would be. He ran up the steps, as the tune of *John Brown's Body* came at full blast through the window, which was open a few inches at the top. He let himself in, and the roar was enough to deafen him. The sitting-room door was open, and he walked along and peered in.

Zebadiah, standing with his back to the window, was conducting the choir and contributing with a fine baritone. Homer, next to him, was singing tenor. Elvira sat on the arm of the chair which had been bought especially for Dawlish. Gregg was in it; Gregg had a mouth-organ at his lips, and was playing the melody extremely well. Tim and Felicity sat opposite him, singing with the rest, Tim's deep bass reaching astonishing depths.

Tankards and glasses were on the tables. There were the remains of some sandwiches and savouries which they had obviously bought while they were out. In the fire-place were screwed-up balls of newspaper, so greasy that Dawlish suspected fish and chips; a faint smell bore out his suspicions.

They finished *John Brown's Body*.

Zebadiah tapped the table with his tankard.

"Quiet, please! We'll have *Yankee Doodle Dandy*—can you remember that tune, Charley?"

"Sure, sure," said Gregg, in a voice so markedly American that Elvira screamed with laughter and patted his cheek, and even Homer grinned, "*Yankee Doodle Dandy*—like this, isn't it?"

Gregg, obviously expert on the harmonica, played the air, and the others started to sing. No one had yet seen Dawlish, who drew a deep breath and came in on the second bar.

Elvira and Felicity faltered; none of the men paused for a moment.

Dawlish's voice became the loudest of them all.

"Well, Pat," said Zebadiah, putting an arm round Dawlish's shoulders, "I'm real glad things have worked out over here. I should have hated any constraint between us. We didn't see things quite the same way, I guess. I'll admit that if you hadn't acted so fast, I don't think we should have got the results—we should still be worrying about the next attack. You happy about it, now?"

Dawlish smiled brightly.

"I'm always happy. Not about Meyer, but—" He shrugged. "He'll have his lawyers."

"Yes." Zebadiah frowned. "When the New York police have cleared up the mystery of the trouble over there, I'd be really happy, too."

The telephone bell rang. Felicity answered.

Homer, Elvira, and Gregg had already left; Gregg had managed to arrange an hotel for them, and Zebadiah was to follow. It was now nearly one o'clock, and Zebadiah was looking tired. Tim was sitting back in an easy-chair, smoking, smothering yawn after yawn. Dawlish hadn't yet had a confidential word with him, but Tim would have found an opportunity to say had anything gone wrong.

"Hallo," said Felicity. "Yes—yes, hold on." She held the receiver towards Zebadiah. "For you, Uncle Zeb."

"I guess that's the Embassy," said Zebadiah. "I gave them this number." He took the receiver. "Deverall speaking. . . . Yes." His voice sharpened. "Oh, I see, thanks. . . . Sure, that'll be fine. We can fix it. . . . Sure, the only way. Good-bye." He rang off, and laughed. "Trouble with the Clipper, but I can fix it. I guess I'd better be getting along. Felicity, I haven't had time to tell you that I think you're swell. Just swell!"

Felicity laughed it off.

Zebadiah drove off with his luggage, which Elvira had brought up from Haslemere in the hired car. The Dawlish's watched the red light disappear, and went back into the flat. Tim stood up and yawned. Felicity asked a question with her eyes, and Tim grinned lazily.

"Perfect! I got her there, saw Bill, and he's fixing it. With luck you'll have a provisional report in the morning. *Now*, I'm going to bed."

"Good idea," said Dawlish.

He felt dog-tired, but didn't drop off to sleep at once. Felicity, already asleep, slept snug and warm next to him. She'd had little to say; she had been worried, too, and wished that Dawlish was not so certain that they hadn't seen the end of the affair yet. He could just see her profile, in the light from the mews. He realized that while a thing like this was on the go, she lived minute by minute, often in fear. She had been afraid, this time, in case her relatives weren't all they seemed. Was she still afraid of that?

He stopped thinking of Felicity. Trivett hadn't been on the telephone, and if Bligh had reported to the Yard, Trivett would have started to raise hell.

So far, so good.

He wished Rosa's case-history hadn't been so impressive to look at.

He was dozing, and suddenly became rigid. A faint sound

penetrated his consciousness, and was repeated. He pushed back the bedclothes and crept out of bed; and the sound, of metal scraping on metal, came again. He reached the bedroom door. It was pitch dark in the hall, but he crossed to Tim's room opposite, and slipped inside. The sound came again, and as he put a hand on Tim's shoulder, to wake him, he thought he heard another; of a window, opening. The only window which could easily be approached from the mews was that of the living-room. All the doors of the flat had been left open; that was why the sound had travelled so clearly.

Tim woke.

"What is it?" he whispered.

"Visitors. Be ready for trouble, I'm going back to bed. I'd like to know what they want."

Dawlish moved into the hall—and heard a different sound, as if someone had knocked against a chair or a table. He slipped into his bedroom, closed the door, and climbed back into bed.

Less than a minute afterwards, the handle of his door turned.

TWENTY-FIVE

SURPRISE PACKET

The shadowy figure of a man was visible in the doorway, thanks to the light from the mews. Dawlish, tightening his grip on the gun, was prepared almost for anything, and had the reassuring knowledge that Tim was ready for action.

The burglar's face was covered by a scarf or mask; Dawlish could just pick out his eyes and the trilby hat pulled low over his forehead. Dawlish expected a torch to shine; it didn't. The man came forward stealthily, and it was hard to believe what happened next, for the man went slowly down on his knees. He was a yard from the side of the bed, and appeared to be looking at it intently.

Dawlish wasn't sure what happened in the next few moments. He could hear the man's breathing—soft, regular. Then the intruder straightened up, still a yard from the bed. Dawlish, grip now relaxed, watched through his lashes. The man turned round and went out, pulling the door to softly behind him.

Throughout all this, Felicity slept.

Dawlish pushed the bedclothes back again, climbed out of bed, and went to the door. As he touched the handle, he heard a sharp exclamation outside; before he could open the door the roar of a shot came loud and clear.

Felicity woke in a flash. "*Pat!*"

Dawlish pulled at the door, saw a light and Tim, on the floor on the threshold of his bedroom. There was a heavy thudding, of footsteps, and the sound of the bolts at the front door being pulled back. He knew that the man there would be turned towards the passage, the gun poised. He edged his way towards the passage, and Felicity, sitting up in bed, gasped:

"Pat, be careful!"

Tim was on the floor, unmoving.

Dawlish darted forward and caught a glimpse of the intruder by the open front door, his gun pointed this way. Two shots roared, and the flashes were almost simultaneous. Dawlish fired again and dodged back out of sight. He heard the man running down the steps.

"Careful, Pat!" screamed Felicity.

"Look after Tim," Dawlish called.

He ran to the door, and as he opened it, saw the fleeing man near the exit to the mews. He fired, twice. The man staggered but didn't stop. The stone steps struck cold to Dawlish's feet, and he stubbed a toe. It nearly made him fall. The man disappeared, and as Dawlish reached the foot of the steps, the engine of a car started up. Dawlish ran gingerly, reached the archway and turned in time to see the car swinging round a corner.

He didn't shoot again.

He turned back to the house, walking very carefully, and in the hall light which Felicity had switched on saw that the little toe of his left foot was bleeding.

Felicity straightened up from Tim's door.

"I don't think it's much," she said. "It's in the side of the head. I'll get some water."

She hurried to the kitchen, bare-footed, and in a pale-green nylon night-dress, a filmy thing which clung to her long, shapely figure. The kitchen-light went on.

Tim was lying flat, and there was a little blood at the left side of his head. Dawlish went down on one knee, as Tim's eyelids flickered. Felicity was right; it had been a lucky break for Tim. The bullet had grazed his left temple; at worst, he would have a headache and a sore spot. Dawlish stood up, and Felicity came hurrying, water slopping over the side of a basin. She also had a sponge.

"Get some towels," she said. "Oh—he's coming round. It's all right, Tim, nothing to worry about."

"Eh?" grunted Tim, dazedly. "What?"

"It's all right, don't worry," said Felicity, and set to work with the sponge.

Dawlish fetched the towels and the oddments Felicity would need from the bathroom, and then went farther into Tim's long, narrow bedroom. The bullet had hit first the dressing-table, then the wall, and fallen to the floor. Dawlish picked it up, slipped it into the pocket of his pyjama-jacket, and hurried into the other bedroom. He stood at the spot where the burglar had knelt down, knelt himself and peered under the bed. He could see nothing but his own and Felicity's slippers. He fetched a torch, and shone the light; he wasn't wrong, there were only four slippers, Felicity's heel-less, his own of brown leather.

"It doesn't add up," he said *sotto voce.*

"What on earth are you doing down there?" demanded Felicity. "And stop talking to yourself."

"Oh, yes. Sorry."

Dawlish straightened up, hooked his slippers out with his right foot, wetted his thumb and rubbed it over the little toe, and then slid his feet into the slippers. The little toe struck something, and pain went through him. "Damn!" he muttered, and drew his foot out, picked the slipper up, and shook it over the bed.

A small cardboard box fell out, and powder trickled from one open end.

Trivett looked at the sodden box, the mass of wet stuff which had once been powder, brushed his hand across his forehead, and looked across at the Yard's explosive expert, who had been called from his bed and had arrived here half an hour earlier.

"What do you make of it, Smithy?"

"Not much doubt," said Chief Inspector Smith. "Fire-powder. We've often come across it before—one of the nice little inventions scientists found to have us wage war properly. Exposure to the air starts it off. A little lot like that would have made the bedroom like a furnace in about five minutes. Sure there's no more in the flat?"

"He only entered one room, apart from this, and we've turned it inside out. He didn't have time to make a hole in the floor or the wall. So that's the lot."

Dawlish was definite, and his expression was bleak. Tim, with a wad of sticking-plaster on his temple, sat in an-easy-chair; Felicity was on her favourite pouffe. Trivett, who had dressed hastily and whose shoes weren't properly done up, looked into Dawlish's eyes, and said heavily:

"It looks as if you may be right, Pat."

"Could be," said Dawlish. "I don't think anyone but the people in this show would have a stab at me now."

"Think it was Bligh?"

"Why guess?" asked Dawlish. "It was someone who preferred me roasted to alive and kicking. And that's a remarkable thing, because—" The blankness went out of his face, and he smiled. "I'll tell you tomorrow, or rather today, at tea-time!"

"You'll tell me now," growled Trivett.

"But if I do," said Dawlish, sweetly, "you will probably want to arrest me. Did you have Meyer's house watched?"

"No. I just gave you your respite. So you do think it was Bligh."

"You know, Bill," said Dawlish dreamily, "I don't know what to think. According to whispers which came to me from a friendly little bird, Gerald Bligh had a visitor tonight, and the visitor knocked him out. Bligh must have suspected that the visitor had a look round, but he didn't report it to the police. Did he?"

Trivett said slowly, "No, he didn't."

"Perhaps the little bird got it all wrong. Have you heard from Simister?"

"No. Why should I?"

"He knew about the unfortunate accident to Bligh. So they must have agreed that it wasn't worth worrying the police, and I don't think they would have agreed, if they hadn't had guilty consciences. Do you?"

Trivett didn't answer. Chief Inspector Smith, who had at first been startled, was now grinning all over a broad face; he had two gold-topped teeth, and they caught the light and flashed brightly.

"Bill," said Dawlish, "you've been very patient. Some would say you've been too patient. But if I were you, I'd have Bligh and Simister watched, from now on. I shouldn't leave Meyer's house unguarded for a moment, but I'd defer taking action. I know the joker at the flat tonight wasn't Simister; he was too big. I think it could have been Bligh, but it didn't have to be. Think you could hold your hand until four o'clock this afternoon?"

Trivett stared at him with bleary eyes for what seemed a long time, and eventually took out a cigarette-case, selected a cigarette with great care, lit it, blew out smoke, and asked:

"Why?"

"Because I really don't think Meyer's the big shot and I think we might have the joker by four, *if* we don't act too soon."

"After all," said Felicity, unexpectedly and vigorously, "Pat has been proved *half*-right, hasn't he? The only thing you can do is to hold Bligh and Simister for questioning, and you can't be sure you'll get any results. They'd almost certainly cook up an alibi, for whoever came. Just do what Pat asks, this once."

She smiled, sweetly.

Trivett growled, "One of these days, you'll get me slung out of the Force. Come on, Smith."

"You'll want this," Dawlish said hastily, and gave him the bullet fired from the intruder's gun.

"The one thing about all this," said Dawlish at half-past seven that morning, when Felicity and he were sitting in Tim's bedroom and all were sipping tea, "is that Bligh and Simister must have known I'd kidnapped Rosa, and presumably they want her back. They'd assume that only we would know where to find her, so—why burn us up?"

Felicity, looking hazy with sleep, didn't try to answer. Tim, heavy-eyed, simply shook his head.

"On the whole, I'd say that Bligh and Simister would *not* try to burn us up, so it was someone else, who doesn't care a fig about Rosa. Puzzle, find the someone. I'd find it much easier to believe that Bligh and Simister decided to get out of the country, and I doubt if they'll be in London at the moment. If they're smart they'll have had a private aeroplane waiting somewhere, and they're probably on the Continent by now."

Felicity finished her tea.

"If it wasn't Bligh or Simister, who on earth would want to kill us, Pat?"

"Not us. Me. Sorry. Your bad luck, if only you'd known when you married me, my sweet." He wasn't fooling, and looked at her steadily. "There's one consolation, it means that you're used to shocks of all kinds. Well, breakfast!" He stood up, quickly. "Have yours in bed, Tim. No sightseeing for you today, I'm afraid. Going out with the relations, Fel?"

"I think I ought to stay and look after Tim."

"Great Scott, *I'm* all right."

Tim was almost indignant.

"All the same, I think Fel's right," said Dawlish. "I fancy Gregg is going to have a field day. And I have to be off early."

"Where are you going?" Felicity asked.

"All over the place," said Dawlish brightly.

He bathed and shaved while Felicity cooked breakfast, and was on the way to the dining-room when the telephone bell rang. He went into the sitting-room, and was not surprised to hear Trivett's voice; there was no hint of censure in it, and Dawlish stood looking out of the window, smiling his secret smile.

"Pat, we've had news of Bligh and Simister," Trivett said. "They left London early this morning; started off in a two-seater monoplane from a private airfield in Hertfordshire and were forced down by engine trouble, over Kent. They crashed—both dead. They'd all the papers they needed, and a small box full of cocaine as part of the luggage. The Kent people are sending the bodies up to London."

Dawlish said softly, "Newspapers know this?"

"I'm afraid so. The Kent people didn't know what the pair was mixed up in, but the Press heard about the plane that crashed, and—well, there it is. Does it matter?"

"Oh, a lot. It won't be in the morning editions, but it will hit the midday papers. Pity. Still, we'll just have to step on it, that's all."

"Step on what?"

"Finding our Big Shot."

He heard Trivett's intake of breath, and it didn't surprise him.

"Now listen, Pat—"

"It *must* be someone else," Dawlish said; and told him why he was sure that neither Bligh nor Simister would have wanted him dead.

Trivett said abruptly, "I don't agree. If Bligh and Simister knew it was all up, they wouldn't care a damn about Rosa Meyer. They'd already run out on her, hadn't they? At most, they used her to fool Meyer. I'm not sure of that yet, not sure Meyer isn't involved, but—Bligh's the most likely man to have put that fire bomb under your bed."

"I'll bet you ten to one he knew nothing about it. Bill, zero hour is four o'clock. Let's stick to it."

He didn't wait for Trivett to answer, but rang off and hurried into the dining-room. Felicity began to serve bacon and eggs from the hot-plate. Dawlish ate heartily and was dabbing his lips with a table napkin when the telephone bell rang again.

Felicity sat still.

"Shall I go?" she asked sweetly.

"No, thanks."

Dawlish kissed her on the forehead as he went out, lifted the telephone, and heard a girl say formally:

"Mr. Dawlish, please."

"Dawlish speaking."

"Good morning, Mr. Dawlish, will you hold on for a moment? Dr. Farningham would like to speak to you."

TWENTY-SIX

ROSA

"Hallo, Pat," said Bill Farningham, brightly. "It didn't take us as long as we expected. The patient's still unconscious, but she'll be round in a couple of hours. If you care to get her home, you'd better come or send round for her right away."

Dawlish said tensely, "Yes. What's the verdict?"

Farningham chuckled.

"She's as healthy a girl as you'll find in England. There isn't a touch of T.B., and there never has been, unless I'm greatly mistaken. I rushed everything through, and persuaded Humbleby to come and have a look at her and the X-ray plates. He's quite the best man in Europe on T.B. I didn't tell him the story, but he looked down his nose when I said that T.B. had been diagnosed. There's one serious thing, of course, and we'll have to face up to that later."

"Ah, yes. Simister."

"That's right. Any man who can treat this girl for T.B., or pretend to be doing it, wants a severe jolt. We can go for Simister in a big way. Don't get me wrong, Pat. I've done what you asked, but I can't let it stop at that, although it needn't interfere with what you're doing now."

"No," said Dawlish softly. "It needn't, because I think the job's nearly finished. Thanks, Bill, more than I can say. No shadow of doubt about any of this?"

"Not the remotest shadow of doubt."

"Fine," said Dawlish. "As for the patient—when she comes round, how will she be?"

"She ought to go to bed for a few hours. The dope won't give her much of a hangover. She won't know what's happened to her, and she'll simply think that she slept for a long time. If you mean, can you question her—yes, as freely as you like. She isn't ill, she's a healthy young animal. She might have been persuaded that she's ill, and it could have some psychological effect, of course, but you'll be a fair judge of that. If you're worried, get Robertson or one of the other psychiatrists to have a look at her. Anything about her to suggest a neurosis, as far as you know?"

"No, I shouldn't say there is," said Dawlish. "Bill, do one more thing."

"Yes?"

"Have her sent out by ambulance—Ted Beresford's place will do. She can be taken inside, and then I'll take her away again later, and bring her here. No one will wonder what an ambulance is doing here, then, and she'll be able to come round more or less under her own steam. Can you?"

"All right," said Farningham.

Dawlish put the receiver down softly, beamed broadly out of the window, clapped his hands together with a report like a pistol shot, and then actually chuckled aloud. He looked delighted, his expression was almost seraphic.

He did not know that Felicity had been at the door while he had been talking, or that she was now looking at him darkly. She came forward, and he caught sight of her out of the corner of his eye, swung round, and before she could back away, lifted her by the waist and held her so high that her head almost touched the ceiling.

"Idiot! Put me down!"

"You ought always to be higher than I am, then I could look up to you properly."

"Pat, you fool! I'll fall."

"Only against my manly bosom." Dawlish lowered her, hugged her, kissed her, and stood her aside, but still held her waist; it was a slim waist, and his great fingers almost spanned it. "Darling, I love you, and I've some wonderful news. Rosa Meyer is *not* ill."

Felicity said coldly, "I knew it was something to do with another woman. Yesterday it was Elvira. Today, it's Rosa. The only place where you're safe is at Haslemere."

"Nothing and nowhere is safe from your relations," grinned Dawlish. "Cast the green out of your eyes, my sweet, and get the spare room ready. I mean, the room we were in last night. Rosa's probably coming to stay. You will have to look after her. She won't need nursing, just a sweet and understanding womanliness, the kind of thing you do so well because it comes naturally. If she's a bit bored, let Tim in for five minutes at a time, he'll love it."

Dawlish took his hands away from Felicity's waist, and Felicity frowned up into his face. Felicity had none of the superb loveliness of Rosa Meyer, but for him she had beauty. He loved the golden flecks in her green-grey eyes, the hair which would not always go where she wanted it, her full lips, the tip of her nose.

He kissed it.

"Pat, *must* we have her here?"

"Only for a little while. A very little while. Great Scott, I must go! Be a honey, telephone Joan Beresford for me. Tell her that I'll be along as soon as I can. If she gets an unconscious girl delivered on a stretcher from a St. Mede's ambulance, she should show no surprise at all, just take the patient in and wait for word from me."

"I suppose I'll have to," said Felicity. "The trouble is that you have your own way too much. *Far* too much. First Trivett, now me. You're hopelessly spoiled."

"Keep it up," said Dawlish. "I love it."

He went out, after a few cheery words with Tim, but hadn't started the car engine when Felicity called him back.

"Telephone, Pat!"

He ran up the stairs.

"It's Bowdy," said Felicity. "P.C. Bowdy, I wonder what he wants."

"There's a lot of quality in Bowdy." Dawlish hurried to the telephone. "Hallo, Bowdy."

"*Good* morning, sir," said Bowdy. "I thought you would like to know the result of a little experiment I carried out. I have Mr. Allen's permission to tell you. You recall that I found some cigarette-stubs near the spot where Mr. Homer parked his car?"

"Yes."

"I found another stub, of a cigarette of American make, a Camel, on a later search. It had blown under some leaves. I had it tested, sir. Analytically, I mean. It contained a strong proportion of marihuana."

"A Camel?" breathed Dawlish. "That's exactly what I wanted to know."

At the American Embassy Harding looked across his desk at him with a broad smile, adjusted his red-and-white spotted tie, offered cigarettes, and said he understood that the breach between Dawlish and Zebadiah Deverall had been healed.

"There never was one, except when Zeb was hot-tempered,"

said Dawlish. "I can't guarantee there won't be trouble between me and the family. My wife thinks Elvira is a hussy. I rather like Elvira. So Homer Deverall is F.B.I.?"

Harding's eyebrows shot up.

"Trivett tell you that?"

"I was M.I.5 myself for a long time, and might find my way back. Yes. I shall keep it to myself. And everyone's happy, the dope-ring is broken, the Deveralls go home in two days' time—"

"They're going this evening."

"Oh," said Dawlish. "So they couldn't put the aircraft off."

"They put it off and put it on again. I've had a word with Zebadiah, this morning. He's feeling sick, and staying in bed. That fellow Gregg is taking Elvira out for more sightseeing until this afternoon, and they leave London at six o'clock. There's a special plane going back, and room's been made for them."

"Well, well." Dawlish looked sad. "Er—could I ask a favour? A very small favour. I seem to be asking for nothing else, these days, but I think you'll be able to stand up to it."

"Shoot."

"Can you have a word with the night operator who was on duty at the switchboard here, last night?"

Harding frowned.

"Surely. Why?"

"Just to ask one question—when he's on the line."

"How you love your mystery," said Harding.

He lifted the receiver, asked to be put through to the night operator, who would be home by now, put the receiver back, and managed to avoid asking for an explanation. The call came through in three minutes.

"May I?" asked Dawlish, and stretched his hand out for the receiver.

Harding let him have it.

"*Good* morning," said Dawlish, to the man at the other end of the line. "I'm awfully sorry to worry you. I know you want to go to bed, but there's an important little query about last night. You were on the switchboard between twelve and one o'clock, I take it?"

"Sure," said a man with a faint American accent.

"Did you put many calls through?"

"Not so many."

"Did you call Mr. Zebadiah Deverall, at a Mayfair number?"

"No, sir," said the operator emphatically. "I should remember if I'd called Mr. Deverall. No one wanted him."

"You didn't leave the switchboard, so that someone else would put the call through?"

"I was off for half an hour at three-thirty. Otherwise, I was there all the time."

"Thanks," said Dawlish. "Thanks very much, operator. Good-bye."

"Good-bye, sir."

When Dawlish finished, Harding was frowning. He toyed with the ends of his bow again, watched the almost fatuous expression on Dawlish's face, and said slowly:

"What *is* all this?"

Dawlish raised his hands high.

"It's shocking, but I don't think my Felicity's Uncle Zeb always tells the truth. He said that he had a call from the Embassy when he was at my flat last night, and now I know he didn't. I think I'll go and have a word with Uncle Zeb. Trivett did tell me what hotel he's at."

"Grand Palace. But Dawlish—"

"I know, I know. Zebadiah Deverall is beyond reproach. All the same, he lied, and we ought to know why. May I use your telephone again?"

He stretched out for the receiver, and a wary Harding watched him as he put in a call for the Yard, waited until it came through, waited while he held on for Trivett; it wasn't a long wait.

"Bill?"

"You again? *Now* what is it?"

"Bill, could you find out whether Zebadiah Deverall was at his hotel all last night? That is, from the time he reached it, soon after one o'clock. Night staff and all that, but it's urgent. Really urgent. He's decided to leave the country on the first available plane, and I shouldn't like him to go until this show is finished."

Trivett said, "You're not suspecting *Deverall*."

"Oh, but I am," said Dawlish. "I'm suspecting Uncle Zeb of a lot of queer things, some of them nasty. Like to hear why?"

Vernon C. Harding, his eyes narrowed to slits, mouth set very tightly, watched Dawlish's inane smile, but didn't speak. He took a cigarette out of a Camel packet and lit it, slowly, flicking a match from a book of matches with his thumbnail. All this, while Dawlish waited for Trivett's reaction, and had to wait a long time, because Trivett was recovering from a shock.

Trivett spoke at last: "You're crazy!"

"Oh, yes, nothing new about me being crazy. Still, look at some facts. First, the family arrived at my place and were attacked but *not* hurt. They could have been attacked anywhere on the road, could almost certainly have been killed by anyone with the daring that Corby and Bligh showed. Yet they waited until everyone was snugly at Four Ways. Why? Because I had to be impressed by the danger Zeb was in. Only it might not have been Zeb in danger—it might have been his F.B.I. son, who opened that parcel with the dope in it. Follow?"

Trivett grunted, "Go on."

"Thanks. A little later, Meyer called, and I sent Homer after him. Just before, Zebadiah had slipped a pack of Camels into Homer's pocket. Homer was surprised he had them. Homer followed Meyer, and then things happened to him on the road. Corby and Thomas Bligh were responsible for that. I think it worked this way. Homer was to be killed—or framed. The attack failed. Then the attackers saw Meyer talking to Homer, and played a quick one—to draw attention to Meyer. They'd expect the police to ask who else *but* Meyer would try to prevent himself from being followed? That was a fake. Now, that P.C. Bowdy I told you about has found marihuana in a Camel cigarette-stub which Homer smoked. Zeb gave Homer a pack of Camels because Homer was short. See how it went? Corby and Thomas Bligh's attack was actually on Homer, but I took it to be on Zeb. They then seized their chance to fix Meyer. I brought Uncle Zeb to London. He had a message which made him walk out. He was known to be at Stenway's when Oliver was killed. He was at the dream-parlour. He was then found, having broken out of his bonds, at Meyer's house. Now supposing Uncle Zeb *did* kill Oliver? He would leave his prints, and couldn't escape it being proved that he was there. I was there too soon. So he had to find a way out. He realized that he could frame himself very neatly, and appear to be a stooge for some other murderer. Of Meyer, naturally—who better? I was very doubtful about Uncle Zeb's dramatic appearance at Meyer's house. I mean, people can't gnaw through the ropes that bind 'em very easily. Not even human rats. And anyone so well practised in crime as the supposed kidnappers would tie his hands *behind* his back. According to Uncle Zeb, his were tied in front of him—other-wise, how did he gnaw? Foolish, wasn't it?"

"There could be something in it," said Trivett, "but it's so fantastic that I don't believe it."

"Nor does Vernon C. Harding. He's sitting here looking at me as if I were preparing an attack on the person of the Ambassador. The offence is almost as great, for the owner of Zeb shoes rates high. But remember, Uncle Zeb left the Yard of his own free will. Things had suddenly started getting hot for Uncle Zeb, and he had to do something about it. I'd say that Oliver had discovered he was in the dope business up to his neck, and was about to tell the police.

"Now, some more.

"Having apparently broken out of Meyer's cellar and made it absolutely certain that Meyer would be regarded as the Big Shot, Zeb tried to pick a quarrel with me. Why? I think, to find out whether I was suspicious or not. I showed no suspicion, so we became buddies again. But I refused to take Meyer's guilt for granted. That made me a nuisance. Then, I kidnapped Rosa. *That* made me a danger."

"*Why?*" demanded Trivett, shrilly.

"You'll see. Bligh and Simister knew who took Rosa away, of course. They got into a huddle, and reported it to their boss. Uncle Zeb. Uncle Zeb told them to take what he would probably call a run-out powder. If they flew out, they would draw all the police fire, he wouldn't. Of course, they didn't expect to have engine trouble, that was just too bad. I mean, he wouldn't have put a time-bomb on their plane and made sure of a smash, and so obliterate the evidence, would he? But I think you'll find someone did. Meanwhile Uncle Zeb became pretty sure that I knew more than I should. Otherwise, I wouldn't have kidnapped Rosa. So, he broke into Tim's flat and tried to fire the place. And he was hit by a bullet—I don't know how seriously. He's in bed—just overtired, he says. I don't think he's as tired as that. I think he has a wound, is anxious to get out of the country so that no one here can find out. That's why he's changed his plans. Bill,

I'm going to see Uncle Zeb. I was going to have a chat with Rosa first, but you can do that for me. By the way, did anyone tell you that Rosa hasn't T.B. and that Simister was taking Meyer for a ride over that?"

"Are you—*sure*?" Trivett's voice was faint.

"Yes, Bill. See you at the Grand Palace. Outside. You wouldn't spoil my cosy little chat with Uncle Zeb, would you?"

Outside the hotel, Dawlish and Trivett talked for twenty minutes, and Trivett was helpful. He had already discovered that Zebadiah had left the hotel half an hour before the attack at the flat, and been out for about an hour. On his return he had been limping.

TWENTY-SEVEN

POOR ZEBADIAH

Zebadiah sat up in his bed at the Grand Palace. Gregg had found him a palatial room, and he looked pale but comfortable. He raised a hand in greeting as Dawlish entered, and then waved to a chair. Dawlish sat down and stretched his legs out comfortably, and smiled as if he were delighted to see the American.

"Well, Pat, I'm surely glad to see you looking so well."

"Surprised?" asked Dawlish blandly.

"You've been working at considerable pressure, I guess, and not all men can stand up to that."

"Some of us have the luck," burbled Dawlish. "Luck plays a big part in everything, doesn't it? You can have a run that lasts for half a lifetime, and then one little thing goes wrong, and it's all over. How's your side?"

Zebadiah began to frown.

"My side? What's the matter with my side?"

"Well, it could be your leg or your arm or shoulder—what's the matter with it?"

"I don't understand you, Pat*rick*, you must be imagining things."

"Just like me," said Dawlish. "Felicity is always telling me that if it wasn't for my imagination, I'd lead a drab life. It brightens things up enormously. Where did I wound you, though? Funny how details like that irritate, isn't it?"

Zebadiah hitched himself up a little on his pillows, leaned to one side, and moved his right hand—inside the bedclothes. Dawlish leaned back with his eyes closed and the fatuous grin still on his face.

"That more comfortable? Good! I mean, I know I hit you after you popped the fire-bomb under the bed last night. That wasn't nice of you, Zeb. I mean, you had good reason to hate my guts, but why kill Felicity as well? You ought to have known that I shouldn't like it."

"Have you gone mad?"

"Not quite. Yet." Dawlish glanced at the door, but watched Zebadiah out of the corner of his eyes, saw Zebadiah glance towards the door as well—and sprang up from his chair as if he were operated by steel springs. Before Zebadiah could stop him, he had pulled the bedclothes back, and his fingers closed over Zebadiah's wrist. In the American's hand was an automatic pistol. Dawlish twisted. The other relaxed his hold on the gun, and Dawlish took it away. "A .32—the size of the gun used last night, and—" He opened the magazine. "Two bullets missing. The pieces are all fitting nicely now."

He looked at a patch of blood on the leg of Zebadiah's pyjamas. Dawlish felt it, and the bandage beneath.

"Leg, was it? Did you patch it up yourself, or did Homer help you? The one thing I'm not sure about yet is where Homer comes in. Did he find out you were bad, and turn bad himself? Or is he making sure he has conclusive proof before he talks? Elvira knows nothing about your other business, of course."

Zebadiah didn't speak, but his expression had changed;

malevolence glittered in his eyes. Dawlish put the bedclothes back, and returned to his chair. It was so placed that he could see the bed, the passage door, and a door which led either to the bathroom or another room in the suite. He lit a cigarette.

"Vernon C. Harding can hardly believe it, nor can Trivett. But it's true, Zeb. What I can't understand is why you came to me in the first place. Did Elvira talk you into it, and did you assume I was just a big clot?"

Zebadiah said harshly, "Have you been crazy enough to talk nonsense like this to Harding and Trivett?"

"Oh, yes. Like to hear what I told them?" Dawlish began, watching Zebadiah all the time.

Most of what he said obviously went home. Dawlish had no doubt that he was right, and only the details needed fitting in. He didn't know whether Zebadiah would give him any of the details.

He finished, and stubbed out his cigarette.

"Not bad?" he asked.

Zebadiah said, "If you hadn't told the others, we might have done business, Dawlish."

"No business," said Dawlish sadly. "I shouldn't mind taking a share of the profit you make out of shoes, but when it comes to drugs—oh, no. *Oh*, no. Not a chance. That is, not that kind of chance. Why did you kill Oliver, by the way? Unless you'd like to know my guess about how it all began. Stop me, if I bore you."

Zebadiah didn't speak.

"Right," said Dawlish. "You've been on the U.S.A. end of this drug ring for a long time. Too long. I imagine you began to lose money on shoes, or else you didn't know Wall Street as well as you thought you did, and you started a side-line."

Zebadiah flinched.

"I thought so," said Dawlish. "It was done through the books.

You needed stuff from Europe and the Middle East to mix with your home grown, and obtained these supplies in books which were really drug containers. But Homer was after the dope boys. He got on to Stenway and part of the London end. He opened a parcel, addressed to you, with drugs in it. You pretended to be outraged, faked threats to yourself and attacks on Elvira, and came over here to see what it was all about, hoping to fool Homer. Elvira sold me to Homer, who thought I was good. You didn't agree. You were in a jam, and you had trouble, in London. You thought it would be safe to consult me, put me down as a fool. Stenway had been your agent; you had him killed, because he wasn't reliable and might implicate you, under pressure. You planned cold-bloodedly to kill everyone who was dangerous. Oliver—who worked with Stenway—got on to you. Corby found that out, sent the message which made you leave the Yard, and you went and killed Oliver. Corby also had to die, once he was caught, and you knew he might have squealed, so had a bright idea, which had entered your head after the attack at Four Ways. You began to frame yourself. As I got on to the dream-parlour, you were pretty sure Corby had talked, so your one chance was to make it look as if you were being framed. That story might have stood up with Corby dead, so someone visited me at the flat and killed him. Since then, Gerald Bligh died in an air crash which you fixed. So Bligh couldn't talk, either.

"Simister was in it, too—most dope rings have a doctor. You had plenty on Simister. He'd fleeced Meyer. You knew he was a charlatan and made fortunes out of false diagnosis—a very nasty piece of work, our Dr. Simister. You didn't mind that. Let him work on anybody, let him frighten people to death, let him make a pile out of treating them when they didn't want treatment. Fine—so long as he continued to do what you wanted.

"Meyer was there to take the rap. That's why Stenway always

used books obtained from Meyer, so that if by chance the dope was found, it would look black against Meyer. Stenway used books of little real value, and likely to go through the Customs easily—but sent parcels of valuable books to put up a show with the Customs. And you wanted him to work on Rosa Meyer, didn't you? Why? Just to keep a hold on Meyer? I'm not a bit sure about that, Zeb."

Zebadiah said in a strangled voice, "Where did you get all this? Where?"

"Can't you guess?"

"*She* wouldn't talk," said Zebadiah. "I could rely on her if no one else. She wouldn't talk."

"Rosa?" Dawlish stood up and laughed. "Oh, no—unless she talked in her sleep. In a way, she did. I—"

The telephone bell rang.

Zebadiah started, and stretched his hand out for it. Dawlish turned towards the door, as Zebadiah said, "Hallo," in a hoarse voice. He kept saying hallo; no one was on the line, this was a signal which Dawlish had arranged with Trivett. He sauntered across to the door and opened it—and Rosa Meyer stood there, pale but lovely as a sprite, and dressed in dark blue. Trivett had arranged for her to be here.

"Why, Rosa! Fancy seeing you," said Dawlish brightly. "How nice of you to come and see poor, sick Zebadiah. He was hurt last night, did you know?"

Rosa didn't move.

"What—" she began.

"Come in," said Dawlish, and took her arm, and pulled her into the room.

She stared at Zebadiah as if she couldn't believe her eyes.

"Dear, sweet Rosa, so fond of Rudolph," said Dawlish. "I don't think, my precious. Desperately concerned for Rudolph, but spying on him all the time. He would eat out of your hand, and you knew it. There wasn't a thing in the world he wouldn't do for you, because he thought you were ailing. And all the time you knew the truth. You worked with Bligh, for Uncle Zeb. Stenway had used Meyer for a lot of crooked deals, was always ready to have Meyer framed, if anything went wrong. Meyer was secretive, but you would know if ever he began to suspect the truth.

"And he did.

"He was being blackmailed—about his past, to make him keep mum about what he learned about Stenway and drugs. He daren't go to the police, but came to me. He came just at the right time for Corby and Tom Bligh to begin fixing him. Then things started to misfire badly. Oliver had to be killed, and Corby couldn't be trusted. He had to go—but he'd already told me the truth. I kept an open mind about that, which isn't important now. You came rushing to the flat, pretending to plead for Rudolph, actually to look for him. You looked all right. What's it like to cut a man's throat?"

TWENTY-EIGHT

F.B.I. MAN

Rosa put out her hand, in the way which was so appealing, touched Dawlish's fingers, and held them tightly. She swayed as she looked towards Zebadiah; but if she wanted help from him, she found none. His face was like a mask, and only his eyes showed expression; they were blazing.

Dawlish took his hands away, and brushed them together, as if he were getting rid of dirt.

"Well, Rosa, what was it like?"

"I can't understand you. I thought I was ill. Dr. Simister—"

"Dr. Simister is dead, my pet. And Gerald. But not your Rudolph—if nothing else, he has his life. You did that by having the police take him. There's just one thing I don't get—how did you and Uncle Zeb team up?"

Rosa didn't answer.

"No co-operation at all," sighed Dawlish.

Zebadiah's eyes burned at him.

"You've got some things wrong, Dawlish. I didn't try to have Homer killed. That was Bligh's idea. I called the men off. I wouldn't have my boy killed. I told them I aimed to have him framed as a dopey, and I slipped him the pack of Camels, some of them doped. Then in case they were traced to me, others were substituted later."

"When did you call the men off?"

"I telephoned them at that hotel in Haslemere when you were talking to Meyer."

Dawlish said, "Maybe you did. Oh, well, it'll all come out in Court. Trivett's waiting outside; his patience has to be known to be believed. I'll fetch him."

He turned round.

The door leading to the bathroom opened. Homer stepped in. He held an automatic in his hand, and did not seem concerned because Dawlish also held one. Rosa turned towards him, took a few faltering steps, and then went towards the bed. She dropped down on it, sitting close to the wound on Zebadiah's leg.

"Why, Homer!" breathed Dawlish.

Homer's small, sallow face was set, and like his father's, his eyes were burning.

"I can tell you how he got to know Rosa. They met in New York, four years ago. She was there to see some friends. Here in England she's supposed to be an orphan, but in fact she's not. There was an orphan, who died. Four years ago, Rosa took her place, her passport, everything. Rosa was in New York at that time, and even when she was that young, she was on the fringe of the drug racket. I know. I dug up some facts about Rosa before I came here. I knew she was Meyer's wife, and thought that fixed Meyer. I didn't know how wrong I was.

"It wasn't until this trip I really began to worry. I soon worried plenty. I'd found out that Zeb shoes were being used to distribute drugs in the States *and* overseas. Simister and Bligh began it in England, and Stenway teamed up with them."

"With your father," Dawlish said. "When did you know about that, for certain?"

"Right now," said Homer. "This past day or so I've been worried, but didn't know for sure."

"That's too bad."

"My father controlled most of the supplies, I guess," Homer said wearily. "He owned the so-called cotton estates where marihuana was grown, in the deep south. I've just had word from the States about that. When he caught me with a parcel open, he had to work fast."

Zebadiah's eyes still burned. Rosa put a hand out and touched his, but he didn't seem to notice it. He looked, now, at his son.

"I thought I'd fooled you," he said. "I just had to try."

"Sure, you tried. Even bringing those books, to make it look as if you were going to confront Meyer with them. Just to build up an impression of innocence, for me and Dawlish. Your big mistake was trying to fool Pat. Elvira really finished you, by making you come to Pat. This is going to hit Elvira mighty hard."

No one spoke.

"It's going to hit a lot of people hard," said Homer, and the words seemed forced out of his mouth. "But it's going to break up the dope ring. In that news from Washington, they say they've discovered that one of Zeb factories turns out a certain kind of shoe, and all those shoes have false heels—a new fashion Dad invented. Don't have your shoes mended, have new heels screwed on. You have a dozen operatives, all highly paid, filling the heels with dope. And you've a list of customers, as long as my arm. That's it and all about it, Dad. You did a fine job, Pat."

Dawlish didn't speak.

"Oh, Homer," Rosa said in a weak voice, "you can't mean any harm to your own father. Why don't you forget all about it? Bligh and Simister were bad, bad right through. No one would believe anything *they* said."

"You can hold your breath." Homer was abrupt. He turned to Dawlish. "That right, Trivett's along the hall?"

"Yes."

"Will you go get him?"

Dawlish hesitated, looked into Homer's eyes and saw the pain in them, and turned towards the door. He was outside, when Homer tossed his automatic to the bed, and went into the bathroom. He didn't look into the bedroom, to see what happened. So no one saw Rosa stand up from the bed and put her hands out, beseechingly, as if in a final, hopeless appeal.

He heard the two shots; so did Dawlish and Trivett.

Rosa was lying on the floor, a bullet in her forehead. Zebadiah had put the gun in his mouth, and fired.

Dawlish and Felicity stepped out of the car, outside Four Ways, and stood on the porch, watching the other car coming up the drive. In it were Elvira, Homer, and Gregg—a Gregg who still had half a day of his overdue leave. Dawlish unlocked the door, and then turned to welcome the others, with Felicity.

Elvira looked pale and shocked, but she forced a smile as she passed them. Homer showed the strain much less. Gregg was thoughtful and worried, and couldn't keep his eyes off Elvira.

They went into the drawing-room, and Ethel came bustling in, when Felicity rang the bell.

"Did you ring, ma'am?"

"Tea, Ethel, for all of us," said Felicity.

"It's nearly ready, Ma'am. I had your phone call," said the maid, and stumped out on her sturdy legs.

Elvira took off her hat and pressed her hand against her forehead. Gregg looked anxious.

"Wouldn't you care to rest, Elvira? There's no point in over-doing it, and I'm sure Mrs. Dawlish would be happy to let you stay here for a while."

"As long as you like," said Felicity.

"I'm fine," said Elvira, in a husky voice. "When I've had some tea, I'll be just right. Don't worry about me."

"Sis can take it," Homer said.

"We just have to take it," said Elvira. "I didn't dream of the truth, it was such a shock, but—I suppose it was better the way it ended. By killing himself, Dad admitted everything, and—he saved a trial."

Homer looked at Dawlish, whose face was blank.

"Yes," he said. "It saved a trial, and that's a good thing. There's no one left to try, except Thomas Bligh. There'll be inquests, and a check up on Zeb shoes and Zeb agents, but that'll soon pass. You'll be able to go back home in a few weeks. Stay here, until all the fuss has blown over, Elvira."

Gregg said earnestly, "You ought to, you know. It'll be the best thing for you. Don't you agree, Homer?"

Homer put his head on one side.

"Sure. Get to know England better, Sis. I guess Gregg has some more leave due to him, and he'll show you around when you've had a few days rest here. I have to get back tomorrow. I've a hell of a report to make. If there's one thing I blame myself for, it's for holding back. I was afraid Dad was mixed up in it, but I liked him so much I didn't want to admit it was possible. I knew Dawlish was catching on—I could have killed you, Pat. It was the worst thing that's ever happened in my life, the worst thing that ever could happen. But—it's over."

Elvira said chokily, "I can't help thinking about Rudolph Meyer."

"You needn't," said Dawlish. "It'll hurt him, but he thought she was going to die soon, anyhow. Rudolph will get over it. And he'll stay in England, which is what he really wants to do, and give a lot more money away to charity. I shouldn't worry about him. I saw him this morning. He wasn't too bad."

"That's fine," said Homer.

It was after tea, when the women were upstairs and Gregg, who was unexpectedly interested in the piggery, was being shown around by the odd-job man, that Homer and Dawlish were alone together for the first time since the shooting. Homer lit a cigarette, looked at the glowing tip, and then smiled crookedly at Dawlish.

"Pat, will you tell me something?"

"If I can."

"You knew what I was going to do when I asked you to leave that room, didn't you?"

"I had an idea."

"Why did you let me do it?"

Dawlish said slowly, "There were two reasons. Elvira, Felicity to a degree—they'd both have hated a trial. But the strong reason was Rudolph Meyer. If there'd been a trial, it would have brought out too much horror for him. In a way, Rosa made him happy. She didn't give him anything. She used the supposed illness as an excuse not to lead a normal life, but Rudolph didn't mind that. He loved beauty, and he had something he believed was the most beautiful thing in the world. It was so wonderful; it was more dream than reality. I didn't want to kill that dream altogether. Seeing her suffer would have done that."

Homer was smiling faintly.

"You're good," he said. "You're very good, Pat. I'm proud to know you."

Dawlish said, "Forget it," and stood up and went to the window. Homer saw him stiffen, much as he had when he had first seen Corby in the drive. But this time Dawlish was smiling. Homer joined him at the window, and saw a uniformed figure, topped by a policeman's helmet, cycling steadily up the drive. It was an effort, for it was a warm day, and P.C. Bowdy had a lot of spare weight; he looked like a good-tempered bull.

Dawlish went to the door, with Homer by his side.

"Hallo, Bowdy! Nice of you to come and welcome us home. You're just in time for a cup of tea, I fancy."

"Am I, sir? Very good of you, I'm sure. I'll go round to the back in a minute. I know you're busy, and I don't want to butt in. Just wanted to come and say thanks, Mr. Dawlish."

"Thanks? I've done nothing—"

"Oh, yes, you have," said Bowdy. "Inspector Allen called in at the cottage this morning. Says he understands I would like to get to London. Says that he also understands that if I get through the exams and pass a medical for Scotland Yard, *he* won't stand in my way. As a matter of fact, sir, I understood from him that someone at Scotland Yard had a word with him about it. I'm putting in my application for the Metropolitan Force this very day, sir. So, thank you."

Bowdy held out his hand.

Dawlish took it.

ABOUT THE AUTHOR

John Creasey, born in 1908, was a paramount English crime and science fiction writer who used myriad pseudonyms for more than six hundred novels. He founded the UK Crime Writers' Association in 1953. In 1962, his book *Gideon's Fire* received the Edgar Award for Best Novel from the Mystery Writers of America. Many of the characters featured in Creasey's titles became popular, including George Gideon of Scotland Yard, who was the basis for a subsequent television series and film. Creasey died in Salisbury, UK, in 1973.

THE PATRICK DAWLISH MYSTERIES

FROM OPEN ROAD MEDIA

OPEN ROAD

INTEGRATED MEDIA

Find a full list of our authors and
titles at www.openroadmedia.com

FOLLOW US
@OpenRoadMedia